T0171384

S E X
AND
THE SUBURBS

EJ MASON

BALBOA.
PRESS

A DIVISION OF HAY HOUSE

Balboa Press books may be ordered through booksellers or by contacting:

Balboa Press
A Division of Hay House
1663 Liberty Drive
Bloomington, IN 47403
www.balboapress.com.au
1-(877) 407-4847

ISBN: 978-1-4525-1033-0 (sc)
ISBN: 978-1-4525-1034-7 (e)

Because of the dynamic nature of the Internet, any web addresses or
links contained in this book may have changed since publication and
may no longer be valid. The views expressed in this work are solely those
of the author and do not necessarily reflect the views of the publisher,
and the publisher hereby disclaims any responsibility for them.

This is a work of fiction. All of the characters, names, incidents,
organizations, and dialogue in this novel are either the products
of the author's imagination or are used fictitiously.

Any people depicted in stock imagery provided by Thinkstock are models,
and such images are being used for illustrative purposes only.
Certain stock imagery © Thinkstock.

Printed in the United States of America

Balboa Press rev. date: 6/24/2013

Contents

Love is freedom
LOVE is freedom in togetherness.
Love without freedom of choice
is possessiveness, control, power,
jealousy, ultimatums, demands,
pressure, domination, inequality and
manipulation.
Freedom cleanses the heart of anger,
hurt, and pain and lets true love shine.
"Love with freedom is delicious
ambiguity."

I give this book to you ... and you
as a present from my part,
not just a gift of words but reflections from my heart.

EJ Mason

This book is dedicated to Joan Kathleen Smith.

When you find someone who nourishes your soul, loves you beyond reason, and brings happiness to your life, care enough about yourself to let them into your heart and complement your life.

Acknowledgements

Emma Mason Watt McIntosh Girvin, my darling sweet granny, without you in my life, I would not be the woman I am today. Gone but never, ever forgotten. Here's the very best of my words because "the sound of your voice brightens my day."

The patience of a saint and the heart of an angel, my mentor, my teacher, my hero, my mum, Elizabeth Brown McIntosh Paterson, and the man with the push to do my best, my dad, David Paterson—without you both, I wouldn't be here.

To my dearest children, Angus Robert, Kirsty Jane and Amy Rose, you are my proudest achievements in life. To their dad, who left our family life so he could have his own, for not believing I could do this, here it is. Thank you for accusing me of having an affair. You were right! I had an affair with my dream of writing this book.

To my darling brothers, Iain and Douglas, thank you for teaching me all about sticking up for myself and being there when I needed you most and for making me become the best sister you both ever will have.

To my family, Uncle John, Auntie Molly, Auntie Kate, Auntie Ann, and late Uncle Bill, you are the best people to have on my side. To my delightful cousins and families, Fiona, Catriona, Morag, Mairi, Saul, late Jamie, Selina, Mark, Neville, Lindsay, and Tammy. Thank you! I love you all.

To my dearest friends, the family I chose ALL OF YOU ARE MY BFF, Julie, Mark, Sandy, Kellie, Kylie, Julie S, "Uncle Steve", Nat, Nadene, Suzie, Paula, and Lee, Peter and Pippa, Brands, Richardsons; Whallins, Mahoneys, the cocktail night girls, Sunday lunch girls, you have all inspired me and made this possible with belief, love, care, arguments, and opinions. At the end of the day, I feel blessed and special to have you and your families as part of my life. To my old "frienemies" Colin and Jenny, thank you for leaving my life, proving to me you never wanted to be part of mine for the twenty-plus years we knew each other, and the only regret I have is you are my sons godparents, when you cant show your love and support for his mother, then how can you show love and support for him.

My support team and mentors, the angels with wings under their coats, Aunty Pat (editing), Pam, Sergio, Tanya, Geoff, Wendy, Nat, Shona, Darling Charles, Christie, Peter, Amber, and Rosemary, thank you for your wisdom and support throughout the good times and not-so-great times. Thank you for believing in me and being there when I needed your expertise and opinions.

To Amber Petty, Lainie Anderson, Peter Goers, and Amanda Blair, what an amazing time I shared with you. It was ever-so-brief but an experience I am thankful for.

As crazy as this seems, thank you to my red chair, for holding me up and supporting, me and my self-belief. When you have self-belief anything is possible. I have written this book over seven years and my red chair gave me the energy needed to finish it. The red chair made the impossible, possible. Self-belief and a red chair is education without going to school.

And last but by no means least, to my darling Mr Smith, I found gold in a coal mine. I was swept into the arms of an angel, picked from a place of shattered dreams that had crumbled me to infinite particles of ruin. He held me in times of tornados and the waves that crashed my shore. Although he didn't know he was my hearts challenge, he unlocked my door of true meaning and brought me and my pen to a place of no boundaries, no lies. He lifted me higher than cloud nine yet kept me humble and calm in the chaos of distraction, my tantrums of turmoil and kept me finding resolve. The comfort he gave me is impossible to explain and the endlessness of fear faded faster for me than the setting sun. He is my softly speaking angel in hiding as I spent my time waiting, wondering what is to be for me as I escaped from the twisted untruths my life had been. For his arms wrapped around me invisible to all, he connected me to an unbreakable beautiful release, where the sweet madness of it all, he was the call I needed to now share him with you all. You have not only brought my words to life but made my dream come true, and without you, this would not be possible. So to the delightful, charming, insecure, witty, beautiful, and engaging Mr Smith, a man with a tenacious stubborn character, though a tenderness so warm, giving me sunshine and strength for the rest of my days. He is my shady tree on a hot day and has the purest hidden heart I've ever known. Nothing can break us, history has made us. Thank you times infinity. All my love forever and always sweet angel. I appreciate you beyond words. I am grateful to you beyond gifts, and I love you beyond reason. My love for him is freedom and he is the easiest love I have ever known. With every key stroke I look at the the keyboard and I see you and I are always together. I hope you enjoy knowing him like I do.

From this day on, when I look back on the past, I will smile and say to myself, "I never thought I could do it, but I did. I overcame all the people who tried to bring me down, the naysayers, thank you, so need your love so fuck you all….

And to you and you and you Thank you… you know who you are—EJ

Foreword

Sex and the Suburbs is not the glitz and glamour of Manhattan and the style of New York City. Nor is it a story of Mr Big. It is a story of Mr Smith, a faceless character within our suburbs, our workplaces, our sporting teams, a member of our families, always there in the background. Rent-a-friend, helping hand, BBQ cook, we all know of a Mr Smith in our lives. He enchants us, delights us, hooks us, and appears so confident and happy, but the other person within the man is quite a different story.

Almost disconnected in society, Mr Smith is a corporate manager by day, a lonely heart by night, a single father in life, a black sheep in his family, with outwardly false confidence and laughter to cover his mask of low self-esteem, lack of confidence, and pure aloneness. He is a forgotten member of society outside the nine-to-five office buddies, an ATM machine for his children, and a means to extravagance for his ex-wife. He's trapped, stuck in a time warp, a life unknown to some but real for many. Pride and fear rule his life, not to mention the depression of having no one to talk to on an open and intimate level without the dread of judgement and criticism.

With a trying emotional past, Mr Smith is a man of steely determination and avoidance. He blocks not only emotions but a sense of vulnerability and loses out on happiness. He is troubled by what others think of him, scared to feel, and scared to do anything that may lead him out of his own comfort zone.

Intimacy and love elude him, and although he craves it, he avoids it and defends against it with emotional walls, making him a prisoner of his own heart and soul. Until he meets her—

Mr Smith feels captivated by the suggestive intelligence, inner warmth, and beautiful glow of the sexy, sassy, and delightful Miss Jena Jones. She's a lovely lady who shows kindness and understanding to the timid Mr Smith, and she has a beautiful feminine nature. Although very open and vibrant, little does Mr Smith know, however, the real Miss Jones. It's almost as if she is just as uncertain of her own life.

The two of them explore his fears and her inhibitions as if fate had brought them together. The magnetic seduction and chemistry they share is a tempting, teasing, and irresistibly erotic sensuality. Irrevocable and provocative beyond boundaries, their bond becomes close and intimately erogenous.

Society can forget about any one of us at any time. In fact, we all probably know a Mr Smith and a Miss Jones, but do we ever stop to wonder what it's like for these invisible and interpersonally disconnected people in society?

The book aims to promote awareness of men's mental health and its importance in society. I want to bring the importance and adventure of romance back to man's heart, not flowers and chocolates but a caring appreciation of men's mental and emotional health.

Many men need romance in their hearts to heal and move on productively and healthily. Their emotional and mental health may have been somewhat tortured in the high-pressure, personally disconnected society of today's world. Mr Smith is not alone. Unfortunately, drugs and alcohol have become the masks of protection as well as neglect to admission. We are seeing the younger generation of men accept "bromance," where they open up to their mates, which is a great start; however, a heterosexual man who's Mr Smith's age feels happy when he has romantic feelings for a woman. His testosterone levels rise at this point. Therefore, his prostate gland functions well, but this black dog hangs around his heart, closing off any possibility of romance.

Women, too, want romance, and I'm no exception; however, women expect it from men, and men rarely experience being romanced because of demands and societal expectations. Thus, this disconnect can lead to the cycle of poor health and life choices, bringing about separation and divorce at an increasing rate, two phenomena of epidemic proportion in the modern world.

There is no question that a man desires to have sex on a primal level; however, the question is this: How is his lack of romance in his heart impacting our suburbs, families, workplaces, and community? Mr Smith is inspiring, and he has grace, class, and style. He possesses a selfless attitude to support others he loves before he takes care of his own needs. He finds himself in the rut of his life with anxiety and insecurity, tossing up to help others or himself first, much like that of a dieter choosing to eat cream puffs and carrot sticks within the same meal.

Life is not a TV series of events and drama. It is experience gained from wisdom and interpersonal relationships and interaction with others.

Discover the reality of shared passions, similar lives, and the human touch in knowing Mr Smith, and learn about the exciting challenges of how sex and the suburbs is being historically and heartlessly changed by the impersonal connections of the cyber juggernaut. We are humans not hard drives.

Sometimes

Sometimes we need to let someone go to find out
If they love us enough to come back.

Sometimes we need to say goodbye to find out
How we feel when we next say hello.

Sometimes we need to step back far enough to find out
If someone will step up for us.

Sometimes we need to close the door to find out
If someone will open it for us to come back in.

Sometimes we need to hide away to find out
If someone cares enough to come and find us.

Sometimes we need to help another many times to find
out
If they are strong enough to help themselves.

Sometimes we need to walk away to find out
If someone wants to follow us on our path.

Sometimes we need to say I love you to find out
If we are loved in return.

Sometimes we need to take the chance to hope,
to dream, to love. EJ Mason

CHAPTER 1

The Boy from the Northern Suburbs

I've always been the same. At my age,
I'm not going to change much.

As Mr Smith stood behind Ms Jones, his erection in the centre of her back, he stroked her cool arms. On the balmy night, moving slowly towards her magnificent breasts, he engulfed her with erotic sensation. As he slowly seduced and gently kissed her neck, touching and teasing her erogenous zones with his soft lips, the hair raised all over her body with goose bumps and magic striking her insides. The sexual energy, which had been repressed in both of them, had suddenly been awakened. The touch, the breath, the visualisation stimulated and intensified the need to become a lot more familiar with their mystical nature and explore their sexual boundaries

Jerry Alexander Smith was born on April 18, 1967, in Northern England. At the age of two, he immigrated to South Australia with his parents, Robert and Grace, and his older brother, Thomas.

The family of four moved to the northern suburbs of Adelaide, "the city of churches." Like many people from all over the world in the 1960s, his parents moved to the land of opportunity, the lucky country, for a better, richer, and healthier life for their children.

The northern suburbs were like a little Britain, where immigrants built and bought modest homes, worked in boom industries like manufacturing and trades, formed clubs and communities, built schools for their children, and most importantly, developed a sense of home away from home.

The landscape was barren, but the roads and transport system carried a very similar resemblance to the towns in Britain. The difference was the dusty bush land with wide-open space unlike the terraced homes most of them came from.

From an early age, Jerry was a likeable lad who enjoyed doing boyish things like riding his bike and exploring the neighbourhood. Along with his brother, Thomas, he made many friends with local children. He loved stereotypes, name brands, and pop culture at its best, yet a little rebellious and naughty streak shone through his cheeky sense of humour.

At times, he was overshadowed by the natural talent of his brother, Thomas, whom he adored and admired, as Jerry beleived his brother was perfect in every way. Thomas was his role model and protector, but deep down,

Jerry saw himself as the black sheep of his small and conventional nuclear family. He always felt the need to please people and to be liked as much as his brother was. Little did he realise, however, people did like him, but his low self-esteem and natural shyness caused him to feel like a bit of a loner.

Jerry felt incredibly close to his mother, who adored both of her sons, yet he envied the relationship his brother had with their dad.

Like most working-class families in the northern suburbs, they owned a locally made Holden car. Robert Smith worked at the manufacturing plant, as did many nearby residents. The company supported local jobs and peripheral manufacturing and production industries, and it was also involved in many community projects and social gatherings for its employees and families.

They were incredibly proud people yet modest and friendly, remembering their roots and the reasons they had made the journey to the lucky country half a world away from their own families. Being loyal to their homeland, they displayed the Union Jack flag proudly on shop windows, flagpoles, and bedroom walls, yet they could not display it bigger than they could in their own hearts.

This sense of community and loyalty saw many of these people become members of the local football club, Central Districts, whose nickname was the Dogs. This club became the heart and soul of the community, and many local lads became great players, role models, and legends to the growing community. The club wore the colours of red, blue, and white, the colours of the Union Jack.

Almost all of the population of the northern suburbs knew someone who worked at Holden's, drove a Holden car, and supported the Dogs. These people created a class of their own in modern Australia.

Not only did they bring their own values and community spirit, but they brought their own culture, including favourite family recipes of meat pies and sweet puddings. They also brought the traditional baked beans and eggs, which was almost exclusive to the Celtic Anglo-Saxons. This staple diet was almost as common or popular as the surname Smith.

So Jerry had the culture, the values, the name, and the love of the music of his heritage and his time. The Jam was his favourite band—and almost his obsession— yet the Beatles, the Church, and the Sex Pistols all influenced the young Jerry Smith. His social conditioning was picture-perfect to his community. He was a classic stereotype of his era, almost a replica of every likeable larrikin around him.

Yet deep down inside, he had a yearning to perform and let loose his cheeky, fun-loving nature. His desire to please people and make them laugh with his fresh and fun sense of humour without being undignified was challenging for him. His shyness made him feel uncomfortable and awkward being the centre of attention. He often wondered how he could blend in without offence yet explore his natural talent of performance.

Although his brother, Thomas, and most of the local boys in their early teens were exploring their sporting talents, Jerry's mum recognised his natural talent for performance and took him to acting classes, where he entered the world of dramatic arts.

He was following his heart and love of performance, and being in character brought him confidence. From dressing up like a fairy to being an extra in a local TV miniseries, landing this role was his dream of performance coming to fruition. At such a young, influential age, he enjoyed the experience for what it was with no plans or direction for the choice of a career in the performance industry. Jerry was just a young lad with a friendly, soft, gentle, and fun nature, a person with an incredible imagination. His positive, easy-going attitude made him very popular. With his striking good looks, solid family values, and cheeky sense of humour, he was the perfect catch for a young woman to settle down with.

CHAPTER 2

Society Says So

Freedom lies within us all. Neither fear nor fight will see us fall. With vibe and essence around our hearts, with freedom, we will never part.

As Jerry gently caressed Jena in ways that blew her away, smothering her with sensuality, he freed himself from the charade society had forced on him. His deep desire to find her sweet, hidden pleasure and her passion to rid herself of her shy nature saw him lead her to a place of new euphoria.

———꧁꧂———

Being such a good lad, Jerry had his head screwed on. His path and his future had been mapped out for him. Sure, performance was fun; however, he knew it wouldn't be his career.

His social conditioning saw him finish high school in his cool, brown, Californian jeans, suede desert boots, and brand-name jumper, just the same as every other popular kid wore. If you didn't have the latest, coolest fashion and trends, you didn't fit in with the rest. This style was extremely important for his self-esteem. If you didn't have the natural good looks, you didn't fit in. If you didn't have the perfect nuclear family, you didn't fit in. If you didn't drive a Holden, like meat pies, support the Dogs, like popular British music, and wear the latest fashion, you just didn't fit in. You couldn't be one of the "Joneses" unless your last name was Smith. Society said so. You had fit into the way of life, or you'd get left out altogether. Keeping up with friends and trends was the key to being popular.

So society saw the young Jerry move away from his acting and drama, as he left school and moved into the workforce. With his sense of style along with his natural charisma and people-pleaser character, Jerry chose retail fashion as his industry.

Working in the local shoe shop of a national chain, he became a sales assistant, and he was soon recognised for his flair. He was quickly promoted to store manager. As a responsible young member of society, he impressed everyone with his politeness, customer service, and intelligence.

With natural progression, society said it was time to meet a girl. In his early twenties, society saw Jerry meet and marry Meredith, a nice girl who liked very much to keep up with friends and trends. Once again, society dictated that the young newlyweds, Mr and Mrs Smith, buy a house in the northern suburbs not far from where he had grown up and start a family of their own. The Smiths had become the Joneses, as expected. *Happily ever after* was happening in front of Jerry's eyes.

Before Jerry turned twenty-five, his first child, Ewan James, was born on September 11, 1991. Ewan James was a little boy of his own to love, cherish, adore, and protect forever. He was the apple of his eye and the beginning of a new generation of Smiths in the northern suburbs.

His life was happening as predicted by society, and his love of performance and drama soon became distant memories. No longer could he enjoy a sense of himself as an actor, as he was now a husband, a father, a homeowner, and a manager. The responsibilities of reality became firmly implanted in his everyday living.

With the added responsibility of a family, Jerry felt that he needed a job more secure than the fickle retail industry. He took up a basic role in the post office. The nine-to-five weekday schedule suited family life more than the fun and flexible pace of the retail environment. A responsible father and husband had to have mature, stable employment. After all, in the early '90s, postage was always going to be a necessary part of living.

As Jerry watched his little Ewan James grow, he felt it was time to give him a sibling and create the nuclear family of Mum, Dad, and the two kids, as society had mapped out for him. With the almost perfect timing of being born nearly three years after Ewan James, Jerry's little cherub Kaitlyn Tyler entered the world on July 8, 1994. His family was complete. A pigeon pair, Jerry was extremely grateful for his children, and he loved them

Pretender

You lie you cheat
How do you sleep?
You're not the one you want to be
You cry you weep
Fall at my feet
You don't know who you want to be

Cos you are just a pretender
And you will never change

You are you're not
You're not so hot
You're the only one you've got
You don't you do
You have no clue
You tell yourself what do I do

Cos you are just a pretender
And you will never change
Don't tell me what I want to be
You left me and made me see
Your whole sad life revolves around money

It's you it's me
You could not see
You never really wanted me

It's now it's then
You ask me when
You want me like those other men

Cos you are just a pretender
And you will never change

You could not see
Its was not me
Our lives together could not be
Its over, done
You had your fun
You'll always be your number one

Cos you are just a pretender
And you will never change
Don't tell me what I want to be
You left me and made me see
Your whole sad life revolves around money.

Pretender, you are just a pretender
Pretender, you are just a pretender

Douglas Paterson, Sycamore Road 2007

like he had never loved anyone before. He began to work extra hard to support them as they grew.

On the outside, Jerry, Meredith, Ewan James, and Kaitlyn Tyler Smith looked like the perfect little family. Once upon a time just as the society fairy tale had said where he got a job, met a girl, got engaged, got married, bought a house, had two children, and lived happily ever after. It was no longer a fairy tale; it was reality. He could no longer pretend his life was not what it seemed to others.

As the family grew and the expectation of being one of the Joneses (or Smiths) set in, cracks started to appear as pressure to keep up with friends and trends became heavier and more stressful. Jerry felt he was falling short on meeting Meredith's extravagant needs and constant demands for more. His self-esteem, his energy, and his sense of fun dwindled as her disappointments increased. His efforts became exhausting as Meredith constantly wanted more than they could afford.

Society had said that this was his path, or so he had believed; however, his wife had had other ideas.

CHAPTER 3

Going Home

Life begins at the end of your comfort zone!

Standing in Jerry's room, they stood, touching each other as they both took apprehensive yet yearning breaths. Longing to touch, to feel, to embrace, and to stroke with voyeuristic intentions, they kissed and mentally undressed each other. Anticipation growing with explosive intensity, Jerry felt the warmth of Jena's tongue tingling through his bloodstream to the tip of his raging erection. He now had Jena in a place of comfort, ease, and soothing ambience.

———∽∿∾⟳◉⟲∽∿∾———

While Mr Smith lived in his pressure-cooker life, his mother, Grace, became terminally ill. He was not only dealing with the harsh reality of the demands society was putting on him but also silently grieving his mother's illness.

Find a Way

I hide behind my macho image, a brave face no one can see.
But just below the surface, the scars are trapped, not free.
I am a man of pride, of value, and of worth.
I cannot help but walk away from my family's hallowed turf.

The control continues, and the blame and nastiness remain.
"You need to do what I say, as I hold both the reins."
My children are accustomed with what she expects from me.
Her diamond rings and fancy things, a world no one can see.

The way it's meant to be is not what it seems from here.
My word and honour is ashamed from hostile, bitter fear.
More and more is what she wants. A shallow heart it shows.
Simple things are what I need, some love and care that glows.

I struggle hard, working day and night, to give her all I've got.
With a heavy heart and empty bag, I left her with the lot.
Although I see what she is to me, the mother of my children,
Why can't she see I cannot be controlled by her every whim?

The guilt plays on my mind, my clear and wholesome soul.
Beliefs and hopes have taken a very heavy toll
If I need to spend each day trying to find a way
To give my children what they need, each and every day.

Appearance and impression, the finer things she does crave.
To be like all the rest of them, she expects me to scrimp and save.

Eating toast and jam or cheese and ham, sometimes skipping meals,
I wait for her to call and ask me how it feels.

The call it comes but not for me, just my wallet and my giving.
"I don't care what you do, but you must keep me living."
"I want it all, and I want it now," I hear her bellowing tone,
"Or your children will not see you," as I listen on the phone.

As I reflect and give once more, I know it soon will end.
I will find the answer when I stand up and defend.
For now, I must sit and wait for my children to want just me.
I am their loving dad, giving all my love for free.

The noose around my neck is loose. The change is drawing near.
The bubble will boil and burst, and my children will come first.
Taking tiny steps with my large frame to find a better place,
For love and care will get me there, to shine upon my face.

Because he was so close to her when he was growing up, he felt helpless the sicker she became. The financial stress, the arguments, the expectations, intensified the tension within his marriage. The different upbringings of him and his wife caused Jerry to sink further and further into indecision, depression, and grief.

During this tumultuous time, his mother lost her courageous battle. As the black sheep of the family, Jerry had never felt so alone. His confidence and self-esteem took a dramatic turn for the worse and hit an all-time low.

He needed to make a decision, a decision that would change his life path forever. After all the years of celebrations, good times and bad, the decision lay purely on his shoulders. Guilt consumed him, and he worried about facing judgement and criticism from everyone who knew him.

He knew the dream was over. Society had taken its personal toll and the fairy tale of happily ever after had ended.

His eyes were wide open, his heart was crushed, his darling sweet mum had left his side, and he needed to change it all. He had to walk away from the pressure cooker that life had become and step away from what had been making him so unhappy. All the animosity, expectation, and disappointment, all the wrongs he seemed to have committed, according to his wife, had to end, so he needed to find a way.

So Jerry began to walk the path so bravely to a different disappointment. He walked down a path where no one in his family had walked before him, down the path of separation and divorce and back into the family home to live with his dad, the man he felt he barely knew.

The emotional and mental torture of his married life was relieved, yet he questioned his decision over and over again. He was exhausted and empty, and he had simply fallen out of love, though how dare he seek peace and happiness for himself without shame? Could he have stayed in an unhappy marriage forever? Although he knew the answer to these questions was *no*, he found it incredibly hard to live in his family home, where judgement sat and shame was all around him.

Jerry missed his children terribly but knew he could not stay with their mother in a very unhealthy marriage. It was best that he didn't put them through years of his and Meredith's differences. He felt like the home environment had become toxic to all of them.

Deep down, he knew he was living a lie. Jerry lived a life to please others. He just wanted breathing space from the societal pedestal. His perfect life was not what it seemed. His life of being second to his brother saw him finally put himself and his needs first, but not for the good reason he wanted. Although he adored his brother, Thomas, and he wanted to be just like him most of his life, he realised he was not his brother and set out to be his own man. His fondness of Thomas was clear as his energy glowed when he spoke of him and the bond they shared. Yet he could not bare his soul to him for fear that society would mock his emotions and feelings. Society said real men didn't cry and real men didn't hurt and certainly didn't discuss or deal with their feelings.

Jerry believed people would see "a real man" as weak and that the man would lose his masculinity and strength if he revealed his true emotions. However, Jerry had been conditioned by society. He did not understand that real masculinity was actually in his own power to love, care, and deal with emotions. This myth had plagued his mind, his heart, and his soul for as long as he could remember, and was an inner strength he had neither discovered nor exposed.

However, when he left his marriage to move in with his widowed dad, Robert, with little more than the clothes on his back, Jerry felt a little more at peace, especially because he was back in the home where he had grown up. He had nothing else but peace of mind, though he knew had to rebuild his life now. He also knew he had a second chance to rebuild and re-establish a relationship with his dad.

He was home away from home, and divorce having come and gone made it a little easier being in the comfort of home. Jerry found resolve at work. Having something to do and somewhere to go made his life worthy and productive. He was able to see his children, although Ewan James was being heavily influenced by the nature of his own generation, made him rebel against his family, and steered his life in a very different direction from what Jerry had hoped for his son.

While he was dealing with the heartache of Ewan James's circumstances and choices, Jerry discovered his dad had befriended a local woman. His dad became more and more involved with this woman and her lifestyle, and after a short courtship, Robert announced he was going to marry the woman and move into her house.

With Robert remarried and settling into his new home with his new wife, Jerry was now left home alone. He had everything from furniture to cutlery but no one to share it all with.

He had this home filled with memories of love and abundance, a fondness to comfort him on his nights alone. He came home to silence, no complaints, no noise, no nagging, no hostile arguments, just himself to dine alone, sleep alone, and be alone. This was a life he had not planned, yet this was where his path had led him.

Solace came to Jerry when he shared his travel time to work. He did most things alone, but not travel. For his journey to work, he took public transportation, where he witnessed all the weird and wonderful sights with fellow commuters—people just like him in their own zones with common purposes, travelling from origin A to destination B. Most of his fellow travellers where part of the nine-to-five rat-race city workers. Some were schoolchildren, and some were not going anywhere in particular. However, they huddled together on crowded train carriages during rush hour. Rain, hail, or shine, every different culture, age group, gender, and race faced their Groundhog Day together, yet silently alone. Jerry and his fellow travellers understood each other without a word, just a look and an occasional smile, which gave some of them a sense of belonging somewhere in the world, on the northbound train ride.

But for Jerry, who generally travelled later on Thursdays and Fridays of the pay week—he often gathered for after-work drinks—he saw a different crowd. These commuters appeared lonelier. Perhaps it was because many of them had stayed out for drinks because they had no one or nothing to return home for.

Thursday and Friday night drinks after work were a big part of Jerry's social life. He saw his workmates more as family members. So these late-night train trips saw Jerry either quite tired or so tipsy that he would often fall asleep, missing his stop. Sometimes he would get off at the wrong station and would have a long, wobbly walk home in the darkness of the often risky and tumultuous northern suburbs. In his merry state, he would sometimes lose his way. At times, he would resort to walking along the train tracks that he travelled to guide him homeward.

The train ride into work was his outside world. Through his toughest times, his work was his solace. It was here he could use his talents, connect with people, and feel his worth. He would say to himself, "Just do it, Jerry. Just do as you are told. Just do what society says so. Don't rock the boat. Don't stir the pot. Don't do this. Don't do that—" So with steely determination and perseverance, Jerry jumped through hoops in order to please everyone around him. He clawed his way through workplace changes, office politics, and everything his workplace demanded of him. His work was his whole life, and although it was challenging at times, his work was his comfort zone.

But deep down, Jerry still felt a yearning to be a family man. He knew his marriage had been detrimental to him as a person because he had never felt appreciated or truly loved. He was seen as the provider because society had set him up like this, but he felt he couldn't give someone something he didn't have. He could no longer allow himself to be controlled by a person who wanted more than anything else in a material world. He couldn't be part of the Joneses because he was part of the Smiths. Although he, too, liked the finer things in life, there were limits, and his marriage demanded way too much of him. His own sense of right and wrong had been rocked to the core, and he had to walk away from the expectations his ex-wife had placed on him.

But where was the man, the father who had his two children, son and daughter, the pigeon pair, just as society had said it was going to be? How could he show them his love? With his eldest, Ewan James, rebelling at such a young age, drifting dramatically in his own life, overwhelmingly influenced by young love, and his youngest, Kaitlyn Tyler, growing up so fast and becoming an adult herself, where did he now fit?

He saw his children, though vastly different, were becoming independent and starting out in their own lives, and he felt all he was to them was a person who worked extremely hard to give them and their mother everything they wanted and needed. Jerry was well aware he was sacrificing his own happiness to give to his family, but rarely complained. Nor could he speak up without a fight erupting. He went without so many things so his children and their mother could have it all.

He felt comfortable being around the people he spent the majority of his days with. Holidays from work were a rare thing, as he had very little income to go anywhere, so his days were long at home. Not having anyone to make

Demons hide

I'm sitting here all alone
Waiting here by my phone
Waiting for you to reply

The Heaters on its cold again
The rooftop overflows with rain
And still I hear nothing from you

And then I go to that other level of low
I can't describe this twisting and turning inside

Then I go and think again
Is this the start of just an end?
I'm sitting here thinking of you

The days are melting into one
The winters end and spring has sprung
I'm sitting here thinking of you

And then I go to that other level of low
I can't describe this twisting and turning inside

And here I go again my friend
I hope you will be there in the end
This journey of chapters and trust

My demons clash I can't relax
My head is like a fatal crash
But still I'm here waiting for you

And I just can't feel immune to the possible fall
My demons hide as I'm twisting and turning inside

And I just can't feel immune to the possible fall
My demons hide as I'm twisting and turning inside.

Douglas Paterson—Sycamore Road 2011

plans with or anyone to share daily times with, he chose to isolate himself, so his work was his contribution to his self-esteem every Groundhog Day.

His after-work drinks were an escape and a time to just enjoy himself without the stress and sadness he felt when he was alone. Not one to complain, he buried his feelings deep down, his demons hiding under a warm and giving heart and soul.

CHAPTER 4

Learning to Surf

Although we all have our own paths on our one-way roads, we always find our true friends on that two-way street.

Breaking with tradition, Jerry allowed Jena to lead him to her. His erection drove a visual yet stimulating sensation of wanting to explore her, who outclassed more than he had imagined, as she held the reins of suspense and seduction. Inducing him with her warm pelvic area thrust against him, her persuasion was hypnotic and magnetic. His charm oozed with captivated appeal as she allured him purely with presence.

Although Jerry did not have much motivation, time, or spare money to undertake home renovations, he did have a very creative mind and imagination. He had a hidden talent and style for building furniture. He could do almost anything he put his mind to, yet his ability to express his talent was overshadowed by his lack of self-confidence and self-belief. He was always very concerned about what others thought, and he worried about what they might say.

So his days and nights were quiet. His TV and computer were his company, his best buddies. Football was his favourite program, and when it wasn't football season, he would fill his time with reading. He loved to read the autobiographies of successful people and become inspired by their lives. TV, movies, and books allowed him to lose himself from the stresses and loneliness of his reality. He took time to absorb the different lives of others, gain insights and perceptions, and keep up with current affairs in order to stay entertained.

His computer, however, along with social media, kept him connected with friends and family. Although Jerry was a self-confessed introvert by nature, he had a lovely, confident demeanour, a warm but wicked sense of humour, and a sharp wit that always made people laugh. This side of him was incredibly funny, and it made him very modest yet incredibly sweet and naturally attractive. He hid his nervousness and anxiety behind this confident personality.

His computer and the anonymity of the Internet helped him overcome his nerves. It was a way of staying connected, too. He also enjoyed playing golf from time to time, and he took in a weekly game of volleyball. Jerry was always happy to catch up with people on social media, particularly Mat and his mates, with whom he enjoyed an annual boy's weekend.

Although he spent so much time on his own and appeared to enjoy his own company, he still had a deep yearning to share time with someone special. He was incredibly reluctant to engage in anything meaningful, as his experience, pain, and hurt was at times too torturous to reveal to anyone. The quiet solitude of his lifestyle made it very hard to change his ways, though he had a very clear awareness that his heart was fragile from a broken marriage. This left him vulnerable and sensitive. He felt constantly disappointed, as if he was a failure in his own mind. Dreams and goals were just that, nothing but unattainable things, according to him, as he felt so trapped by expectations. Without his workmates, his father, his brother, Mat, his mates, and his beloved children, Jerry lived quite a solitary life, yet outwardly, he seemed social and confident. No one knew or understood his real feelings as he appeared friendly and happy.

So with the anonymity and expectation-free cyber world, Jerry tried his hand at Internet dating. He had learnt the art of surfing the Internet and took the risk of belonging to social media networks, so he started riding the waves through the many online profiles of women.

The worry, the stress, and the anxiety of constantly wanting to please others plagued his existence. Cyberspace was a place where he felt safe and could guard his heart and use his sense of humour and quick wit to impress the ladies rather than expose his fragile self. As risky as Internet dating was, he was prepared to learn to surf and take the chance.

CHAPTER 5

A Surprising Find

Don't confuse fun with happiness. Fun is short-lived,
but happiness is forever.

Spellbound, Jerry absorbed all of the attention Jena appeared to give him. He wanted to please as well as receive the gorgeous woman, who now lay in front of him. He had to grip his erection to avoid a premature eruption of the strongest desire, hankering lust, and sweetest affection he had felt because of the mysterious girl he had the pleasure of sharing such a sensual experience with. Jena was slipping through his other hand and his mind like he had never known; this experience was so much more than he had ever imagined or planned yet so exquisite and so stimulatingly sexy.

—⟊∿⟊∽⟊⟊∿⟊—

Little did Jerry know what he would find in this new world. A few ladies had caught his eye; however, no one had captured his mind and shone in his heart yet.

His online profile name was reflective of who he was, and his cheeky smile shone on his profile picture. This caught the attention of a shy and introverted girl, a girl with presence who appeared outwardly confident with a bright, attractive mind and wonderfully creative imagination.

Jerry found himself intensely curious yet calm. He felt a wonder that he hadn't felt before. In the social media world and various forums he participated in, he was comfortable around the shy and introverted like himself. He found he could connect with the outside world from his own living room without fear of failure and without being judged. He could share what he chose to share with his mates, family, and friends. He could have those cheeky conversations and delight others with his funny stories and one-liners. He could express his care and compassionate side with his bright personality. But really, who knew the real Jerry Smith?

Jerry had control over his comfort zone, control over his life, and the ability to sign off at any time. He could take time out to think, absorb, and flirt with reality. This brought him a sense of contentment—or so he thought. Using the cyberspace medium stopped anyone from getting too close, which was just the way he liked it, although deep down, he still longed to be loved, appreciated, and respected for who he was—a man, a son, a brother, a father, and a friend. His fear and hurt from the past still often consumed his reality and saw him withdraw from anyone who got too close.

Like many single people his age who were exhausted of the bar and nightclub scene that attracted players and sleazy types, Internet dating appeared like a safe option. Although it did bring a stigma of desperate and dateless in its infancy, it had become a safe and acceptable part of modern society, where all generations could be selective in finding like-minded people.

In the winter of 2010, a surprising find showed up on his profile—Jena Marie Jones, a shy girl from the coastal suburbs of Adelaide. He struck up an intelligent yet cheeky conversation with this anonymous woman. She appeared upbeat, funny, smart, witty, very charismatic, and entirely engaging. She was warm with her words, and she was very in tune to the reality of Internet dating. She gave little away, as Jerry didn't realise she was very curious about this confident, funny, and incredibly good-looking man she was chatting with now.

Jerry felt a connection, yet he was cautious with this unknown girl in the online world. She seemed so confident and smart. Jerry was a little awestruck by her spark and zest for life. She soon became the delightful, sexy, and sassy Miss Jones.

Jena had her own reservations about Internet dating, but she, too, was at a place in her life where fun was a must; even though she knew the risks, she was immersed in her desire to know Jerry. She found him mysterious and mesmerising. She was a girl who liked interpersonal communication and face-to-face contact. But many things played on Jerry's mind.

Jerry had waited for a long time for a second chance, for a break that would make it okay. There was always some reason for him to feel unworthy, and he made it hard at the end of each day. He needed some distraction or a beautiful release. Was Jena his beautiful release? Why did he feel empty and weightless at times? Jena made him feel like he was in the arms of an angel. Talking to her, he felt comfort and warmth, especially when he was away from the stark, cold contrast of his home, where there was only endless lonesome nights.

Was what he felt for Jena sweet madness or glorious sadness awakening inside of him? The feeling almost brought him to his knees. Or was he being pulled from the wreckage of his broken heart and his unresolved silence? All Jena wanted was for Jerry to find that comfort in her arms, as he too needed to find comfort in hers. He wanted to share some of his life with a special woman because it seemed everywhere he turned people greedy for more surrounded him, like vultures circling their next feed.

With this knowledge and experience in his life, he struggled to share his feeling with Jena for fear that her closeness may be too much for him to handle. He revealed that he often made excuses not to attend social functions because he felt so unsure of himself and most of the time didn't have the energy to put on a happy face when he felt so sad inside. His brave face was intended to ensure that others didn't judge him. He would use countless excuses—he was either ill or busy all the time—to avoid attending most social functions. Little did he know that Jena had sensed he was like this and that she didn't want to put any further pressure on him.

But what was so different about Jena that made Jerry increasingly curious about her? What was she hiding? Who was this girl he had only spoke with over the Internet? They both seemed to bounce off each other very well.

Jerry eventually gave Jena his phone number and his address, as they were keen to meet face-to-face. He thought she seemed like a very nice girl, and he obviously felt a sense of ease with her, which encouraged him to give her his contact details. She really was the perfect stranger. All he had was words on a screen and a current photograph. All he could do was trust his own judgement that what she was telling him was true. Was this the art of learning to surf or learning to find the surprise he was looking for?

CHAPTER 6

Sex in the Suburbs

*Be prepared for someone to walk into your life and
turn it into happiness.*

As Jerry found himself caught up in this intimately sexy
rendezvous, Jena found herself not only wrapped in
the arms of an intriguing man but also engrossed in her
own thoughts. *The visuals of touching my silky soft skin and
feeling the pleasurable ruggedness of your body against mine
become real. Your kiss delish, evoking blissful feelings and igniting
a flame deep beneath my skin, while your fingers explore hidden
erotic places and the warm wet wonders of me found in the depths
of my senses, kindling, teasing, and tickling my soul with pure
ecstasy*, she thought.

————————

In the darkness of the night, a fine figure is seen. Is
it real, or is it a dream? Who knows until the touch that

makes hair stand on end? It is a very real feeling where seeing is believing. Then you wake up. Reality bites, and it bites hard, at times in all the right places. That's what is presented, and deal with it you must.

But what better feeling could you ask for than the one at the top? It is euphoria, ecstasy, engaging, exhilarating, inviting, and very much welcoming.

As the dream continues, it is so much more. It is respect, regard, rebellion, the unknown, and almost untouchable, but it is very touchable, tangible, tantalising, and tasteful all in one hit.

And a hit becomes the aim for the home run—to have your needs met with a smile, a laugh, a tickle, a lick, a touch, but most of all, handled with care. Huh?

It doesn't make sense. How can a moment of time change your view on life? How can it change life as you know it and into something completely new but very, very old in the scheme of things? Was it there all along? It definitely was forbidden fruit—the very nature of nature herself—but blossom it must, for natural progress and fruition.

The moment of peak is pure and prime. Do moments like these need just the right time and the right place, ambience, and serenity? They are moments to create, deliver, and remember, for where else would we fantasize?

Fantasy is a place where everything is right. It is a place where you deserve to go. You create it, so if it makes you happy, why not deliver it so you can remember it for what it was, a real fantasy? The soul feels a need to fill the fantasy. Is it fantasy, or is it soulful feelings? Who knows what they are, but we all have them. If we didn't need soulful feelings, could we still fantasise? Imagine a world of soulful feelings? It wouldn't work, but then again, we would have such fewer divorces and such a more peaceful world.

In the depth of the cold, wet winter of 2010, Jerry found himself interstate with work. He was able to stay in contact with those back home through the Internet and telephone. He found himself in the warm and sunny climate of Australia. While he found himself basking in the sunshine, working hard yet enjoying the sights, the fine dining, and the luxurious accommodation, he continued to remain in contact with his newfound online friend, the intriguingly delightful Miss Jena Jones. They exchanged many cheeky and forthright conversations online, and because they had exchanged phone numbers, texting became frequent.

This communication broke a silence for him in a very enlightening way. He soon realised Jena was a great communicator and conversationalist, even though they had never met face-to-face.

On his return, the wintry conditions and quiet life found him alone again. As he had given Jena his address, he plucked up the courage to invite her to his home. He felt comfortable doing so, although he had only invited one girl to his home before. For some reason, he trusted his judgement and instincts with Jena.

She arrived, bright, bubbly, and easy-going with sparkling eyes and a smile to match. Jena was just as confident and talkative as she was online. This made it easy to engage with her instantly. Jerry thought to himself that she seemed quite "normal," for want of a better word.

Jerry sat back in his beanbag, huddled next to the heater for the cold winter's nights. The delightful Miss Jones sat back on the armchair, enjoying his company. She found herself quite taken by the man, whom she had initially thought was fond of boating from the image of his profile picture. She found a charming man with whom she seemed to be quite at ease, sitting in his lounge room, yet she noticed he was also quite reserved. Although this reservation gave her a sense of safety, it also made her feel comfortable and calm. Inside she was struggling a little with her impulsive decision to go to a perfect stranger's house late at night. However, there was a side of her that felt a magnetic force had brought her there. Her sense of apprehension had all but disappeared as she and Jerry enjoyed living the moment of their first face-to-face meeting.

There was an electric vibe in the air and chemistry emerging from both of them, so Jena took the chance and acted on the spark she had felt in the room. She sat down beside him on the beanbag to warm up next to the small radiator. Jerry's house being double brick held the cold inside the walls. The only thing Jena could do to heat up was the most natural thing in the world, engage in body heat. So that was what she did.

Jerry was awestruck by her closeness, and her soft breasts against him almost hypnotised him. Up until that night, he had only seen a headshot photo of Jena. He felt so fortunate to see her in the flesh and incredibly lucky to have her warm up and feel her beside him.

They came together very naturally, and both felt this was an amazing experience, though the best was yet to come. Both of their heart rates were beating so fast, like athletes who had run a marathon. This mix of desire and immense seduction came across them when they locked lips for the first time. It blew Jena's mind, as she had never felt such amazing passion in particular, the anticipation and raw honest approach. Jerry's erotic and romantic magnetism was delightful beyond words or thoughts. He was strikingly handsome and flirty with a seduction that was natural and warm. His sex appeal was so alluring and stimulating to Jena that she felt she was spellbound with fascination and unrestrained excitement. How could a man be so charming, so warm, so sexy, and such a gentleman?

With such an impassioned, fiery vibe in the room, Jena and Jerry forgot about the actual room temperature. They felt their body temperatures reach a boiling point. Jena felt she could no longer resist what Jerry was giving her. This dynamic intimate attention was so erotic yet incredibly tender. The deep, passionate kiss intensified the intimacy as they embraced each other with acceptance. Here were two people from two different worlds meeting together for the first time almost by chance, and they were about to experience a moment never to be forgotten.

What seemed to ignite such a stimulating seductive spark and raw emotion in these two strangers? Why did it seem so significant in an insignificant time and place? Such arousal had instigated an energy neither of them could explain.

Even though both had engaged in the world of Internet dating, they had their reservations. They had not been looking for love as such; however, a little twinge and a loud uninterrupted silence told them perhaps some kind of love had found them.

They both knew their hearts were vulnerable and fragile from past relationships and that they kept themselves under very tight wrapping and behind their high emotional walls. But the natural instinct and mutual attraction for each other took over their closed feelings, and the progression of desirable, sensual, explosive sexual intimacy set in.

Jerry was physically strong, and his suggestive moves touched Jena in a place of pure delight. His body was oozing sex appeal, and attraction was so persuasive that he was able to paralyse Jena with pure ecstasy. Jena had never felt this before. Something inside her sent a shooting signal to the place in her mind where she locked off this one amazing moment in her own memory vault. It crossed all her personal boundaries, unwrapped many feelings and all but tore down every brick in her solid wall.

As Jerry softly kissed her neck with little intimate pecks, he touched all of her erogenous zones as he had never before. He then moved down her soft body to her amazing breasts, and he was awestruck by their sensual softness. He gently kissed and nibbled her perfectly hard nipples and held them ever-so-gently in his masculine hands. Jena felt his hands cup her breasts and handled them with such care and caressed them ever-so-softly with his sweet lips and tantalizing tongue. It was such a heavenly feeling. Jena felt aroused beyond anything she had felt before.

Unbeknownst to Jena, Jerry was incredibly stimulated by this experience. As Jena sat upon his hips, she had captured Jerry in a moment of time. Nature could take its course for both of them. It appeared that time stood still as Jena slid upon Jerry's hard erection. He felt her warm and wet feminine body surround him. The fit was perfect, almost as if they had been made for each other.

This intimate moment was a memory neither of them felt they would forget. Although it was spontaneous, no other moment appeared to be more ideal—right time, right place, right people, right moment. This was not just sex for one night only; it seemed much too good for that.

Jena had let go of all her inhibitions, which Jerry knew nothing about. In fact, he knew very little about Jena's past. Her fear of being intimidated or humiliated all but disappeared.

Jerry seemed to feel so comfortable in his own skin and so taken by Jena's charisma and sensual intimacy he, too, let go of his shyness and introverted personality. He was open, extremely giving, and most pleasurable. His masculine body and strong character were awesome and sexually delightful. From his strong hands to his luscious lips, from his tantalising tongue to his fit body, he was the complete package.

In the throes of delightful ecstasy, the entry and re-entry created a mind-blowing experience. From a truly connected state, they succumbed to an orgasmic state of euphoria. The room temperature had escalated to the same level as the vibe in the air.

As they both came down from living this moment with each other, it soon came time for Jena to leave. A night of fun, temptation, anticipation, warmth, laughter, and, of course, the intimate sexual experience had all come to an end.

Jena knew she would never forget it. At a time where she wanted the delightful male company of Jerry, meeting him face-to-face was more than she had ever dreamed of. A smile would remain bright inside her for a long time to come. This moment was a memory she would hold with her for the rest of her life. She knew that Jerry might never know why it meant so much to her and how much this night would change her life.

CHAPTER 7

At Arm's Length

Patience, respect, and time will never fail us. Step back, step out, step aside, step forward. Patience, respect, and time will never fail us.

The passionate intensity ensured Jerry's aroused male senses attracted him slowly down to taste the exquisite, sweet, aromatic flavour of femininity. Anticipation and intellectual foreplay expired as the subtle and elusive hint of stimulation and seduction saw him and Jena's bodies and minds entwined, waiting, wanting, needing. A romantic flavour of lust and what appeared to be the beginning of something so much more mixed, showing true colours, sensations, hunger, and vulnerable exposure.

⎯⎯⎯~᙮᙭᙮᙭⎯⎯⎯

After that magical moment on that cold winter's night and a parting offer of catching up again for a movie,

The Power of Choice

"Please help me," I say from the core of my soul,
Which is battered and bruised from the hideous control.
Domestic violence is terrorism in the home and the heart.
It is the most suppressed kind of torture I know.

Abuse doesn't always come in a loud, roaring tone.
It is sanctimoniously delivered as he whispers in my ear.
It's not sweet nothings as though it would appear.
It's horrific. It's cruel. It's crippling and mean.
It's destruction, dysfunction, all controlled by fear.

The silence is piercing, and terrorism is imminent.
Like waiting on the plate for the ball to be pitched,
No idea of direction, speed, or strength.
On guard, I wait to cover my base.

The curve ball from left is what I expect.
The attack so severe, the defence so weak,
Moments of fear, destruction, and torture,
"Your tears are a weapon" as I cry and not speak.

Strike one. I'm down and nowhere to run.
Face the onslaught of what's about to take place
Reading the play, as it churns in my soul,
"You have no credibility." I miss again to save face.

Strike two. I beg, yet not on my knees,
Time ticking by with anticipation high.

Power and control are reigning supreme.
"You will not scream," but I will not lie.

Strike three. I'm out. It's time to go.
The punishing silence, the push, the pain.
Game over, I choose life over death.
"It's my life," I say, and my safety will remain.

Its starts up again as I leave the ballpark.
The memories, the injustice, the right to survive,
In the lounge room, the bedroom, the courtroom, I pray.
With children and scars, I thank God we're alive.

With dread, fright, and panic that his lawyers instil,
These bullying tactics are no longer to be.
Change is essential, and focus I must
As others have sacrificed the ultimate before me.

Entrapment beckons with lawyers in tow,
But no one to stand up and say it is wrong,
Only me to decide what is to be,
The road being tedious, tumultuous, insidious, and long.

Growing tired and exhausted, weary and sore,
With no money left to pay the huge legal bill,
Nothing to hide and proud to be me,
All I have is my children, my dignity, and my will.

With chains and roadblocks, it doesn't matter anymore.
I've been through the tunnels of torment before,
With my children alongside in the darkness of horror,
Change on the cusp of what is in store.

A writer I am, no fear in my words.
Erin Brockovich, Bono, or Geldof I'm not.
Just a brave little person breaking the silence
On a life of fear, intimidation, and violence.

With courage, I stride, gathering kindness from many.
Speak up, I will for me to grow tall.
My heart in tatters, my spirit crushed,
Trying to stop the pain of it all.

For my children and me,
We wear no shame.
We are wholesome and good,
Not scapegoats for blame.

The silence is broken; the wisdom is known.
The barriers removed, the door no longer shut,
There's no turning back in the darkest of tunnels.
It's too black to reveal the deepest of cuts.

In a world of self-battles, delusion, and grandeur,
The terrorist lives on, though not on TV.
It takes strength, courage, and the will to survive.
Plus, the power of choice to say,
"No! *He's not living with me.*"

Strike me once, I chose to cry in pain.
Strike me twice, I chose to run and save face.
Strike me three times, I chose to walk the safety path
with my children, my pride and my battered soul to
fight for our freedom.
Strike me never again.

Jerry thought of what had happened. He had met the delightful, sassy, and sexy Miss Jones., but this made him unsure of his own life. This created a dreadful feeling of uncertainty inside him, one that made it so hard to block out his reality.

In the weeks that followed that fantastic night of passion and sensuality, contact started to wane between him and Jena. He couldn't bring himself to put in effort for fear of failing and her rejecting him. His insecurities and low self-esteem gripped him yet again. Guilt and a sense of failure from his broken marriage consumed him. Eventually, contact with Jena came to a halt. Jerry remained shy and reserved to the detriment of his happiness, getting along with his Groundhog Day life. Jena became a distant yet delightful memory. Although they only lived ten kilometres apart, the emotional distance was significantly worlds apart, according to Jerry. Little did he know that Jena, too, was feeling something very similar.

Jena had become a girl Jerry remembered, but he was out of touch with her. He didn't really know what she was up to in her own life or what path she was travelling. He had not followed up on the movie offer, and she hadn't asked. She had made no contact.

Jerry knew that Jena had great potential, and he had been very surprised to find a lovely woman was single. She was a gorgeous, giving, smart, strong, and beautiful woman.

Unbeknown to Jerry, the delightful, sassy, and sexy Miss Jones had been suffering her own uncertainties. She had endured an horrific divorce involving violence and manipulation. She had been subjected to playing her role in society of living with a husband known as a "home devil street angel." She had been controlled by the power of his choices, and she had worn a very brave face most of her adult life.

Jena needed to find herself, enjoy her life, and find her safety and security in her own heart and mind. She was still single because she would not allow someone to mistreat her like that again. Her single life was her choice, and men she had met had not been prepared to respect her and her own space. She was more interested in using her mind and showing her free spirit and kind soul in her own time. So as long as Jena saw her single dating life as fun to protect her intimate self from harm, she was happy.

Making time to give her life a complete makeover that involved renovating her house, reconnecting with friends and family she had so dearly missed—these short-term solutions helped her remain focussed. Jena was such a generous girl that she would share her last dollar or last meal to make sure the people she loved had something. Giving away and sharing her possessions was her way of living a happier, more complete life. Thoughtfulness and kindness gave her a sense of self-belief, something she had missing in her life for such a long time. Her loving nature and giving love with no expectations of return had been stifled and entrapped in a loveless marriage. But her ultimate value in life was forgiveness, something her grandmother and mother had taught her. Jena learnt to forgive herself if she felt disappointed or let down by others.

She felt almost immune to empty and broken promises along with meaningless words. People had betrayed her trust for years. But caring about people was her nature. Her closest friends, Sam, Julia, Kerin, Marcus, Kate, Richard, and Jesse, were her rocks. They remained true and trustworthy. She had also met a man who was beginning to manipulate her. He would tell her that she was the epitome of womanhood but then yet fucked with prostitutes and other women to try to make her jealous. Her friends stood up and stepped in to protect her from this predator. She felt very ashamed of herself for allowing such disrespect. In the end, Jena came to her senses and broke away from this man and his abhorrent behaviour.

So as the contact with Jerry became less and less frequent, Jena felt it was time to let go of the possibility of ever seeing him again. Although she thought about him often, she believed he had forgotten all about her and that perhaps that beautiful moment they had shared hadn't been as special to him as it had been to her.

Jena found her own resolve yet again and pushed on with her life. A new job, a new car, and a sense of independence gave her life new meaning. Her family and friends were unswerving in support for her. She learnt to look after her heart and soul with everything she had and everyone around her. She had inner beauty and outer charisma to embrace a new life, but she also maintained an underlying wall of vulnerability and caution.

Although Jena had tested her flirtatious zest and spunk with Jerry and shared some intimate secrets, she still felt a sense of trust with him. She had only ever met him once, but her instinctive awareness and lessening of fear told her he was a lovely guy. Perhaps it was their timing that didn't match. However, as she hadn't heard from him in quite a few months, she had resigned herself to Jerry being a missed opportunity. She let go of any possibility of ever seeing him again, as the lack of contact indicated his lack of interest.

Little did Jena realise that Jerry had kept her number. He often thought about her and her intimate beauty. He lay in bed at night, wanting to contact her, but his lack of confidence saw him do nothing. His hesitation at times tormented his imagination.

Jerry continued with his Ground Hog Day routine life. Being a football supporter, he followed the team with pride, and he was always there during their successful and not-so-successful times. The loyal, working-class, blue-collar brigade were loud and proud as the year 2010 saw the Doggies in yet another league grand final and belief in the area was at an all-time high. Like many thousands, Jerry knew they would win, and he celebrated with the loyal fans into the wee hours. True to form, the text messages were clogging up phone networks as many sent out bragging rights to the 2010 grand finalists. "Go, you Dogs," had been sent to everyone in certain contact lists. The message went out to everyone, and Jerry was no exception. With a heart full of pride and that winning feeling along with many beers, all of Jerry's phone contacts got the message.

Although not a Central supporter, Jena was an avid football follower and had heard on the radio that the Dogs had claimed the trophy. She received a message on her phone "Go, you Dogs" from an unknown number. She figured it was from her cousin, another Maddog supporter. Not for one moment did she think it was from

Jerry. Little did Jena realise that the infinite distance between her and Jerry had disappeared in a single text message. She figured her cousin had sent the message to everyone in his phone, as he would have been absolutely thrilled with the results and he was probably celebrating like mad dogs and Englishmen.

However, not realising this message was from Mr Jerry Smith, Jena continued living her newfound life with ongoing love and support of her family and friends. Although she had often thought about the fond memory, the delightful moment, the wonderful night, and the amazing feeling she had shared with Jerry, Jena just locked it away in her memory as a wonderful once-in-a-lifetime experience that was too good to be real. Maybe he remembered. Maybe he didn't. Life went on.

Blissfully unaware and caught up in redecorating her room one Saturday afternoon, around a month after the "Go, you Dogs" text message, Jena received another message. That was nothing unusual because she often received many on a daily basis, friends and family dropping lines to say hi or making arrangements. When she looked at her phone it was just a number, which made her curious. This number had no name attached to it as she opened the message. It read, "Hi, Jena, I really enjoyed our beautiful moment and still get immense pleasure of the memory and meeting you. I hope all is well with you and thank you again. Jerry."

Jena had to sit down because she was a little overwhelmed. A rush of excitement filled her body. Jerry had not forgotten her. He had not deleted her number either. She realised she had made a lasting impression with the charming Jerry, one good enough for a follow-up message, albeit six months later. Jena didn't quite know what to think, if anything. She then realised the "Go, you Dogs" message had been from Jerry. So throwing caution to the wind, she replied with a polite yet cheerful hello. She couldn't believe he remembered that moment they had shared.

The text chat continued, and Jerry asked her if she was still single. He couldn't believe his luck when she said yes. He confidently asked her out for a drink. The distance Jerry had created between them had all but disappeared. Jena felt flattered and humbled by Jerry's thoughts of her. She was delighted he had contacted her again.

With their connection re-established, albeit mostly by texts and e-mails, once again technology helped the shy Jerry and the dynamic Jena get to know each other on a more regular basis. Although they lived separate lives, they shared daily thoughts and experiences to help them understand each other and grow comfortable with each other's personalities.

CHAPTER 8

Knowing Mr Smith

So as I begin to reflect on myself and what I see in others, some may be offended, and some may be grateful. Whatever the outcome, it's about being vulnerably honest, a trait that has been neglected by mirrors of true reflection.

His sexual and most pleasurable trait was his raw and open self-honesty and the connection allowed him to soothe her passion with sweet flowing desire. They fell into their hopeless dreaming state of seeing and touching each other souls as well her tenderly stroking his hard throbbing penis with one hand gently massaging his testicles with the other. The gentleness of her hand and softness of her grip was, overwhelmingly, the moment he wished time could stand still. Never before had he been touched in this way, no grabbing no pulling just a beautiful seductive feminine touch. His body was in a euphoric state of reality. This was no fantasy it was a breath taking experience with him wanting more as he

A laugh and a smile

Each day, I wonder, Will I hear from him ?
Each day, I wait for some kind of sign.
Each day, I think, Will it be now?
Each day, I feel he is biding his time.

Each moment, I share a laugh and a smile.
Each moment, I wish to bring him near.
Each moment, I hear his laughter and pride.
Each moment, I feel my heart beat clear.

He is an angel sent from above
To teach me that I can truly love.
He brings me fun, not sorrow or pain,
An enigma of sorts again and again.

found himself dancing to her rhythm with every caressing stroke. This was no masquerade ball for pretenders, no hiding behind masks, as their bodies and souls were revealed to each other.

———

The adorable and incredibly funny Jerry gave Jena millions of reasons to smile and make her heart sing, her soul dance, and her spirit shine. He was tempting and teasing yet amazingly thoughtful and sweet. Jena kept him on his toes with her own quick wit and cheeky messages. She was upfront and daring, though soft and feminine as well.

Jerry, though, still remained an enigma to a degree and a little hesitant in locking in a date to catch up. Eventually, Jena asked, "So what does a girl have to do to have that drink with you?"

"Details. Details," was his reply. He appeared to be in no hurry to see her again.

Her self-doubt started to creep into her mind. Was he just leading her on or playing with her feelings. She was becoming frustrated. The sense of fun was wearing on her reality, but something told her to hang in there and give him a chance, knowing he was shy and a little low on confidence.

So Christmas 2010 and New Year's 2011 began with only texts as communication between the two. Once again, Jena felt Jerry had forgotten about his offer to catch up. Nevertheless, Jena went on her summer holiday down the coast, happy and content to have some fun in the sun.

Knowing It's Time

*Afraid to tell you how much I love you in case you don't feel
the same,*
*Afraid to say I would like you to be mine in case you don't
want me to be yours,*
Scared of speaking up in case I get rejected and hurt,
Risking my heart in case it's worth it,
Knowing it's time.

*Say you can see me with you; I'm afraid of the excitement it
brings inside.*
Say I've always been there as a choice of love interest of mine.
Know who I am to you; I'm afraid to believe.
Risk your own heart in case it's worth it.
Now I know it's time.

No longer afraid to say it out loud,
Love interest of mine, handsome and fine,
No longer hiding under my bed,
Great to be free from that fear and foe.

Free to be me and say how I feel in case you do feel the same,
Ready for togetherness, a kindred soul in my life,
Accepting my values of what I hold dear,
Been patient, kind, offered love and tenderness all for you.
Knowing it's time.

No longer uncertain of affection we share,
Ready to see opportunity arise,
On the cusp of your horizon, fearing nothing to hide,
Warmth fills me up, knowing it's time.

No longer afraid to say it out loud,
Love interest of mine, handsome and fine,
No longer hiding under my bed,
Great to be free from that fear and foe.
Knowing it's time, now I know it's time.

She shared her time with her family and close friends, surfed, and relaxed on the beach. Jerry wasn't far from her thoughts, but he was hundreds of miles away and kept at arm's length.

It was almost as if society said once more that they weren't meant to be together or see each other again, but her feelings of happiness overwhelmed her when she thought of him. "Damn society," she would often say to herself. He had made her feel so happy and made her smile so much brighter with a laugh and a smile. The sun shone warmer during the day, and the stars sparkled whiter at night, all thanks to the enigmatic Jerry Smith who brought fun to her life.

On the last day of her holidays, knowing she was heading home that day, Jena rose with the sun. She strolled along the beach with a few other early risers walking peacefully, taking it all in. With the silent, beaming sunrise and the soft white sand under her feet, she sat and contemplated what the year ahead and her future would hold for her. With the year in its infancy, it was time to make some plans to move forward in her life. No longer was she going to allow others to manipulate her and she was also going to accept what she could not change but commit to her own choices and decisions.

So as the sun started burning the back of her neck, it was time to head back and pack for the trip home. All in the house were still asleep, so she quietly cleaned and packed what she could. During this time, she heard a message on her phone, but she continued cleaning. Something told her it could be important, so she sat on the balcony with a coffee and read her message. It was Jerry asking her to catch up that morning. Her heart sank, as she knew it wasn't possible. She was hundreds of miles away and wouldn't be back in the city until the afternoon. After all this time of waiting for the date that never came, it was here, and Jena couldn't make it. Was this the sign she had been waiting for? Jena replied and told him that she couldn't make it. Disappointed but keeping true to herself and her commitment she had made earlier that morning, Jena accepted it wasn't meant to be. Plus, if Jerry was serious, he would suggest another time. Jerry replied and said that he had plans that afternoon. This was the sign they weren't meant to be—or so she thought.

Jena continued cleaning and packing, and she enjoyed one quick swim in the ocean before she hit the road. The week along the coast had reinvigorated Jena and given her a new perspective on life, the boost she needed. She felt a little flattened by the inability to see Jerry that day, but acceptance was Jena's resolve.

While she was letting her family know what time she would be home, a message from Jerry came through. To her shock and amazement, Jerry had rearranged his day to meet up with her that afternoon. The gesture had made her feel fantastic, and she had to contain her excitement to focus on the road trip home.

Jena knew she would be cutting things close to meet Jerry at a local café by the beach near her home. She certainly wouldn't have time to change out of her beach clothes. She would have to see Jerry just as she was. Jena never pretended to be anyone but herself. As they had shared such an intimate moment the last time they had seen each other, Jena was a little nervous.

Would the strong and sensual feelings that she had felt that night still be there, or would she feel differently? How would Jerry act with her? These along with many other feelings and thoughts consumed her mind during her trip home. Jena knew it was best that Jerry saw the natural girl she was, unpretentious and with her own sense of self.

The trip took longer than she had expected, and Jena got to the café half an hour late. She fully expected that Jerry had already left. She looked in the café where they had planned to meet and couldn't see him, so she walked towards the beach to enjoy some sunshine again. All of a sudden, a man stood in her way. She looked up, and there he was. Jerry cut a fine figure and looked incredibly handsome, wearing a beaming smile and greeting her with a cheeky hello. At that moment, Jena realised that neither of them had seen each other in the light of day.

Jena was truly taken aback and completely mesmerised by his presence. He was tall, and he towered over her. He even held the door open to the café. They sat at a table for two and ordered coffee. As they sat and chatted, it was almost as if there was no one else there. They got caught up entirely in their own enchanting conversation. The chemistry and spark between them worked just as well, if not better than the first night they met, like some kind of magic. They spoke about everything from family to work and mostly their common interests in football, books, and music.

While two hours passed in the coffee shop, they decided to take a walk along the beach and enjoy the rest of the day. They continued to make general conversation until that awkward moment arrived when Jerry asked Jena if she would ever marry again. Her heart sank, and her tongue got caught in her mouth. She wanted to avoid such an open question. She didn't want to discuss her future with a man she had only ever met in person once before. Marriage for her was almost taboo subject. Jena hadn't wanted to think about commitment to anyone but herself and her family. She had very mixed thoughts about it. Although she believed in an equal relationship, marriage was not necessarily for her. With the silence almost deafening, even though it lasted for only a few seconds, Jena just blurted out, "It would have to be with the right person … at the right time for the right reasons." She hoped this would satisfy his curiosity. The last thing she wanted to do was disclose her controlling and manipulative ex-husband. She knew she didn't want to get married because society said so.

Jerry asked what the reasons would be. Wow, Jena was speechless, so she just said it would be nice to have someone who saw a relationship as equal, someone who had similar interests, and most of all, someone she trusted to confide in. The one thing she didn't want to say was that she wanted someone to acknowledge and value her enough to share her life. She accepted that everyone was unique and that differences were all part of acceptance; however, abusing power in a relationship was not what she was looking for. She felt she needed to have someone in her corner through good times and bad.

It was an enlightening conversation; she realised she had never opened up about these issues to anyone before, yet Jerry made her feel so comfortable talking about them. It was now her turn to ask questions.

Jena turned to Jerry and asked him if he was still on the Internet dating site and if he had met any interesting women or been on any dates. Jena's curiosity didn't seem to faze him as she openly told him she felt the Internet dating game was full of sex maniacs, smutty charmers, liars, and cheating husbands. Players, losers, users, and abusers were the types she had experienced, and she wondered what the females were like. Jerry openly told her that he was still on the site, as there were a few women he enjoyed chatting online with, but he added he hadn't met up with any of them.

Jena felt a little special that Jerry had made an effort that day to change his plans for her, and she realised he must have been slightly interested to move out of his comfort zone to get to know her. Although she was very guarded and cautious, Jena did feel that sense of calm around him, and a little wave of jealousy came over her when she heard that Jerry was still engaging somewhat with other women.

However, Jena had worked so hard on her self-esteem and felt empowered by the fact she was unique within herself. She had nothing to prove to Jerry or anyone else. She was a great person with a kind and loving heart, and it would be totally up to Jerry whether he wanted to see her again or not.

Letters from the Mirror

Yes, that's right. We all look in the mirror and see physical, superficial, outer shells. We fail to see the real images that make us who we really are. We fail to see the actions and words we create with our thinking. We fail to see what we really want to say for fear of judgement and criticism. We fail to see our souls and the purpose of our lives. We only see the competition we create for ourselves. Survival of the fittest perhaps; however, the fittest don't always survive. It's those with poor health who are normally the survivors.

We have mirrors to reflect ourselves, but should we use them to reflect the outer shell, the outer beauty?

When people are disfigured from birth or through horrific accidents, they avoid mirrors. What they are actually avoiding is not the physical scars but the shame the scars represent. We all have scars to some degree. Those who don't think they have any are liars or in denial. They repress them for fear of being exposed as weak. From my perspective, these are the people with no or little conscience and are a result of either trauma and hurt or are born with significant faults so that they really don't know the difference between strengths and weaknesses.

> *So as I begin to reflect on myself and what
> I see in others, some may be offended, and some
> may be grateful for what they read. Whatever
> the outcome, it's about being vulnerably honest,
> a trait that has been neglected by mirrors of true
> reflection.*

As they both enjoyed the warm summer day, the beauty of the beach, and the walk on the soft sand, they realised without words that they had a natural attraction to each other. Their conversation was effortless. They appeared sincere, genuine, and unpretentious. Although it was only their second face-to-face meeting, they seemed to be on the same wavelength of life. The similarities seemed parallel, and their differences were logical, particularly their cautiousness with each other. Jerry's enchanting and charismatic sense of humour captured Jena just like it had on the night they had first met and shared such a wonderful moment in time. Only this meeting, there was no sex and no privacy, but they certainly had the same level of intimacy and mutual affection. Jena instinctively sensed Jerry felt the same way. They were both people pleasers who felt like black sheep in a white flock.

By the time they reached their cars, Jena couldn't wait to see Jerry again, and she hoped he would contact her soon. The striking and impressive Jerry had brought Jena slightly out of her own comfort zone like a chick out of its nest when learning to fly for the first time. He had accomplished what no one had managed to do before.

When they parted, he gave her a simple kiss on the cheek and said that they should meet up for a drink sometime. It had been six months since their first meeting; however, both now acknowledged it was well worth the wait. After all, being naked with someone is not taking our clothes off, it's bearing our heart and soul, disclosing our strengths and weaknesses, and sharing hopes and dreams. However, this would be the first and last time they would meet in public.

CHAPTER 9

Under the Bed

Whether things are looking up or things are looking down …
or we are looking straight ahead, do we see acceptance?

Her visuals and engrossed thoughts were suddenly coming to life. He gently stroked her soft skin, removing her lingerie; he explored her body with his fingers, hands, lips, and tongue. With her back now arched and goosebumps flooding her body, Jena suddenly felt fully encapsulated by the warm and alluring Jerry as she embraced a sense of belonging. His flirtatious ways had her smitten and hooked. Attraction to the lush and lust of voluptuousness was a pleasure for both of them. They could no longer resist the tantalising temptation of sexual intimacy.

————⁓⚬⦿⟠⦿⚬⁓————

After the coffee shop meeting at the beach, contact by text became regular. Jena became freer and opened herself up to Jerry. She had only ever been so open with her nearest friends and closest family. Her timidity lessened, and she approached her newfound friendship with boldness. Although she proceeded with extreme caution, she embraced her feelings. Her past had taught her to be aware of people's actions towards her, yet her natural zest for life and opportunity sat well with her warm personality. She had strong beliefs in humanity and fairness, many that often clashed with some people.

Jerry would say such lovely things to her, expressing his likeness for and fondness of the sassy, sexy, and delightful Jena he was beginning to know. Though shy, he crossed boundaries he had never crossed before. He sent flirtatious and engaging messages with sincerity. His honesty and acceptance of his own vulnerability often saw him withdraw from people as soon as he felt they were getting too close. Yet Jerry saw rawness in Jena he had never seen before in a woman. He, too, felt cautious; however, Jena had caught him unaware, and he secretly wanted to know more about her. He was perplexed as to how she had such an engaging effect on him and why he was allowing her so near.

So as he kept his distance, unbeknownst to Jena, she kept him to his word and asked when they would share the drink he had offered that day at the beach. She had no idea he was holding back because of his lack of confidence. However, on one warm night, he mustered up the courage to invite her to share a drink at his place.

Jena was well aware of what had happened the last time she had been at Jerry's house. She knew, though, that she very much wanted to get to know Jerry outside the bedroom. She certainly didn't want Jerry to think she was only a girl who was exploring her sexual needs or that she was exploiting him to meet her own desires. She wanted an easy, comfortable path to get to know Jerry in reality, not fantasy.

They sat outside on the balmy night, enjoying a few drinks, discussing everything from religion to politics to society and boundaries. This friendly conversation was relaxed, both of them enjoying an evening of warm company and weather to match.

As Jena held self-respect in very high regard, she shared some of her hopes and dreams about what she wanted out of her life. However, the chemistry that seemed to ignite between them was not far from her thoughts. No matter how much she thought, nothing stopped the feeling that Jerry would make her feel incredibly happy if he would wrap his strong arms around her, sweep her off her feet, and make passionate love to her. She tried in vain to stop thinking like this. Her fantasy and reality were crossing over. How could she handle this intense feeling without breaking her own boundaries? It was sex, she said to herself, as there was no way a man she barely knew would make love to her. How could they make love if they weren't in love? How could both of them, being aware of their guardedness and protective natures, endure such passion and excitement?

However, the law of attraction and electricity overruled their thought processes and crossed every boundary that each had and broke down their protective guards with just one amazing kiss goodbye. As much as either of them tried to remain calm, nature took its course.

Jerry's brilliant aura and penetrating charisma mesmerised Jena. He swept her off to his bedroom to share a beautiful moment. Time stood still. Nothing mattered. Jerry caressed every part of Jena, including her mind. He caught her completely by surprise, yet she found herself being open and zealous. This mutual decision found them more vulnerable than they had ever been before. They felt the same as their bodies bonded in every way, and they felt synchronised as they embraced each other's touch. Jena wanted the world and time stop. She thought she could feel this way for eternity. They shared intimate secrets. Inhibitions were forgotten, and they experienced a beautiful moment once more.

They teased and touched erogenous zones with an overflow of orgasmic proportions. They were in pure ecstasy and captivated by the spontaneity of the moment. It seemed impossible to express their closeness in words. Although hours had passed, this enchanted moment seemed to be over in no time, and yet again their guards were up, particularly Jerry's. Jena intuitively sensed Jerry's protective nature was holding him back, because she, too, had felt it in the past. Being frightened of heartache and pain, withdrawal and backing off in the subconscious world for both of them was part of their make-up. Although Jena knew sex changed the dynamics of any relationship, she did feel that what she and Jerry had experienced was more than sex; they had shared an experience that neither of them had known before. Containing her excitement and maintaining her protection was extremely difficult as Jena left that night.

From then on, the contact became less frequent as Jerry began withdrawing from Jena, leaving her with doubts about herself and wondering what she had done to drive him away. But underneath, Jena knew she was doing the same, fearing feelings. However, Jena still felt a very strong inkling. There was much more to learn from Jerry, as she still wanted to get to know the enigmatic man. She felt frustrated, not so much with Jerry but with herself. She felt that there was something very special; however, her outer conscience knew her own guard and protective mechanisms.

Jena found the courage to ask Jerry what he wanted, not only from her but from life itself. Her nerves of steel felt like liquid chocolate as she awaited his response. His reply wasn't as shocking as she had thought it would be. She had sensed his withdrawal, yet she didn't expect he had sensed hers.

Jerry told her that he was wrong and that he thought he was ready for a relationship, but he wasn't. "It's not you. It's me," he said. At that point, Jena realised he had no idea that she, too, felt the same way. In fact, she had wanted to reply with the same: "It's not you. It's me." Their insecurities tied them to each other, and their similarities were clearly obvious.

The only difference was that Jena was willing to get to know Jerry, whereas he wanted to hide under the bed and nip their bond in the bud. It appeared Jerry wanted no more contact at all, as he indicated that everything between them was over. Just like that—a text was all

Enticing Moments

The ol' chestnut rears its head.
"It's not you. It's me," is all to be said.
The attraction and lure turns to cold,
Transforming to dust not like pure gold.

Fascinating appeal being felt inside.
Desirable needs fed from pride.
The ego is struck with hurt and pain.
My revolving door is here again.

Magnetism spinning out of control,
Avoiding temptation is now my role.
Enticing moments flash in my mind.
"It's you, not me," one of a kind.

Pleasure is pain. It's what I know well.
You had me under a captivating spell.
A magnetic embrace draws me in once more,
Inviting charm, just like before.

Jena had. A few words on a screen. As upset as this made her, she felt there was more to it, and she wasn't quite as willing to give up just yet.

Jena herself needed to address her own fears and anxiety about being close to anyone. She wasn't about to give up on herself, and she needed to find the answers she needed for such a short, sharp closure. Jerry withdrew because she was getting too close, and he wanted to shut any feeling out of his life. The last thing he wanted was to expose his vulnerability.

Although uncertainty plagued her mind, Jena focussed on her own protective measures and remained true to herself. She considered her own needs and put her guard up once again. With a secure set of values and self-respect, she drew on the love and kindness she gave Jerry, even though he made it clear he didn't want a connection. She didn't know, though, whether he didn't want one with anyone or he just didn't want one with her.

As time went on and contact waned, Jena grounded herself yet again. Her loyal family and friends, particularly Sam and Marcus, gave her the support, love and compassion she needed. Giving flowers to those near and dear to her on Valentine's Day kept her unselfish and thoughtful. In the back of her mind, however, she wanted to show Jerry how he, too, could be a part of her life. Jena knew how much he had made a difference in her life, but it had to be his choice to accept her.

So with contact now almost ground to a halt, Jena sensed Jerry was suffering in silence—she had an overwhelming feeling all was not well in his life. She knew how reluctant he was to reach out and ask for help or support, so Jena took it upon herself to contact him.

By way of text one Sunday morning, Jena expressed to Jerry that she had sensed all wasn't well. He replied almost instantly and said he was incredibly stressed and worried about big changes in his workplace. The place where Jerry had felt secure was now being shaken up, and he was now facing an uncertain future. Jena offered her support, but unless he told her what was happening, there was nothing she could do.

During their time, Jena told Jerry that she was an insurance consultant and that she had worked within many different industries and that her job included supporting her boss in hiring of employees. She had since left her employment to start up her own business in assisting businesses with risk management and conflict resolution. It was her passion to help people. Jerry had always believed in Jena's intelligence and her abilities. She spoke so well and had a very quick wit, so with this in mind, he asked her if she could help him secure his job. Unbeknownst to Jena, Jerry felt his situation was dire, and in this predicament, he felt almost reliant on another person to assist him, and Jerry put his faith in Jena. They had only shared intimate experiences in the past, and they had never really shared anything serious and possibly life-changing for Jerry.

Jena stepped up with confidence to assist Jerry with his process. The depth of the report Jerry had to produce was intense, and without telling Jerry, Jena herself believed it was beyond her ability. What had she done? She had never undertaken such a complex and difficult job, but her level of commitment and persistence gave her the determination to try. She certainly didn't want to fail at this because of the importance to Jerry, not to mention her own reputation. Although a few weeks earlier, Jerry had all but closed her out of his life, Jena certainly didn't want him to jeopardise his future and job security.

The huge amount of work was overwhelming, but not once could she let Jerry know she had concerns because he was feeling extremely anxious and nervous. Every spare minute, Jena put in insurmountable effort. She wanted Jerry to feel confident and be secure in the work he had devoted his life to, and she knew he desperately needed to stay employed.

Jerry felt uneasy about asking for help. He was so fiercely independent and incredibly reluctant to ask anyone to help him that he felt out of his depth. Jena believed Jerry would see how much she cared about him and would show her his appreciation in some way. She wanted to see how much he valued her help by offering her some down time. Instead, all she got were texts. She had to instigate contact and make time to discuss things with him because he didn't seem to realise the mammoth task that was being undertaken by Jena. She wanted to get this right, and she wanted to make sure she was doing her best work.

At times, her enthusiasm waned as she worked on this. She began to feel very flat, and a sense of apathy was starting to kick in. Jena would contact him because she would need information to get things done. Jerry would make excuses about why he couldn't give her time. She found herself in disbelief when Jerry enjoyed going out with friends, while she worked so hard for him. He certainly didn't seem to have the same level of commitment and sense of urgency as he had expressed to Jena in the beginning.

Without much input, Jena carried on with the information she had. On one occasion while she was hard at work for Jerry, she took a break and accessed her e-mails. She found she had messages from the dating site she hadn't accessed in over a year. When she decided to check these messages, she found that Jerry was online and chatting with other women while Jena was doing his work. She was extremely upset, not only with Jerry enjoying online dating while she was working for him but with herself for being so giving and supportive of someone who clearly didn't feel the same way. What could she do? She believed in doing what she said, and she had committed to helping Jerry and seeing this through to the end. He seemed very comfortable getting on with his life while Jena did his work for him for very little recognition or appreciation apart from the occasional text at her instigation.

Jena felt like a complete fool because he had taken advantage of her. She was torn between her work ethic, her word, her self-respect, and her feelings. She knew she was bitterly hurt, but she ignored her feelings in order to finish what she had started. At one point, she felt so angry and humiliated she wanted to throw it all at him and do nothing else. She hadn't deserved to be treated like this; however, it all came down to her own values.

Her dignity grew stronger, and she continued to give Jerry her full support, her encouragement, and her professionalism. She could not allow her hurt feelings about Jerry continuing to pursue other women and giving them his attention to interfere with her integrity.

Eventually, Jena told Jerry that she needed his input and asked that they meet up as soon as possible. During this meeting, they worked extremely well together as she discovered a very fragile, apprehensive man. Jena found a man who seemed so fearful of his own success yet excited about the prospect of promotion. She found a man who had a warm, gentle demeanour but was incredibly wary of showing it or exposing any kind of self-confidence. He was so concerned with what others thought of him for fear of any retribution and realisation of weakness. She found a man who had rarely been recognised for his talents and abilities and who had put so much pressure on himself to ensure the happiness of others that he forgot about himself. Jerry's path and beliefs had been defined by others and society. She found a man who was so anxious, almost terrified of his own feelings that he was at times scared of his own shadow and his own thoughts. She found a man who really struggled to show her appreciation because he either didn't know how to or didn't want to invite Jena into his space for fear she would see through his macho self. She found a man who had never come across such a thoughtful, considerate, generous, and genuine girl such as Jena Jones. She found a man who felt that sex changed everything, or in his words, "fucked everything up"; however, Jena, who was bold and upfront, told him that it just changed the dynamics.

With this, she walked towards Jerry, gathered her thoughts, and added, "Does this mean that you are not ready for whatever we have and that you will never or don't want to have any further sexual experience with me?"

By this time, Jena and Jerry were almost touching, and the sex appeal was filling the room, oozing out of both of them. The air was thick with anticipation and the chemistry that the two had come to know so well. To Jena's complete surprise, Jerry took her into his arms and kissed her so intensely and embraced her so effortlessly. Jena felt her knees collapse under her. Once again, she was taken.

The two of them were a very hot, steamy, evolving couple. They both shared similar views on relationships as well as familiar paths of their past. The similarities clearly helped them understand each other as well as bond with the desire and magnetism that had brought them together on now several occasions.

Their fondness for each other seemed to grow with time, and the temptation was obvious. No matter what either of them said, they could not stop what was happening between them. Their fear, anxiety, and words could not cause interference. The actions and behaviour spoke the loudest and the same language. It was almost as if they could read each other's minds and finish each other's sentences. There was no fighting the attraction.

That night, they forgot the work as they spent the rest of their time in the bedroom getting to know each other so much better without those awkward moments. The magic spark of Jerry's bedroom made Jena feel wanted. At times, Jena would hear Jerry's words, "It's not you. It's me"; however, these thoughts were so easily displaced by Jerry's affection and the attention he showed her. She felt he did actually want her but just couldn't deal with his feelings and fear of genuine love. These feelings were taboo. Jerry's vibe and eyes said otherwise as Jena watched him embrace the moment. This wasn't just sex. This was a connection that he wanted but just wouldn't allow himself to have.

Why is he doing this? Jena thought. Was Jerry too immature to handle feelings of any nature, or was he totally numb and totally emotionally unavailable? Was he just a player and teaser who wasn't ready for such a fascinating girl? Did he really feel what Jena felt? Did he not want to hurt her, or was it pure fear of failure and inadequacy? Had Jerry never gotten over his ex, and was he still in love with her? Or was he interested in someone else? The questions in Jena's head were endless. She couldn't work out how they bonded so well, yet he was so distant.

Jena began to doubt herself, feeling her own low self-esteem kick in. Many of her friends told her that men are only truly interested when they call and want to make plans, not through sending text messages and avoiding the face-to-face contact. So why didn't he instigate contact? Why didn't he take her to the movies after a year had now passed since their first meeting? Why didn't he ask her out for that drink he had offered at the beach café? Why did he continue to talk to other women on the dating site? Why didn't he seem to care about Jena's feelings? One of her close friends bluntly told her, "He is not interested in you at all, and you are not good enough for him. He is showing no signs of a man who wants to see you or be with you. Just accept that he doesn't like you and is only a friend with benefits on his terms. Jena, you are stupid for allowing him to treat you this way." Jena was so confused because she trusted her feelings; however, the uncertainty had really crept in.

From that point, Jena had to try to unwrap herself and disengage from the lovely Jerry. She felt so foolish and ashamed of herself. Jena knew Jerry was a polite and kind man, and she had seen a sign of real goodness in him. She felt he was just too scared to release his feelings.

However, all the signs pointed to him not being interested in Jena—everything apart from Jena's gut instinct, which told her he was interested and needed more time to get to know her. Trust was a major value both of them needed to develop. Jena did not want to believe that Jerry would lie to her or lead her on.

So with Jerry's work complete, Jena felt she had given him the best chance of impressing his management; however, where did their personal lives sit? After all the inspiring and loving messages and things Jerry had said to her, she wanted Jerry to show interest in her as a woman, not as a professional friend who had helped him out. She secretly hoped flowers would arrive at work or an invitation to dinner would come from Jerry to show his appreciation. But there was nothing, zero, zilch, not a thing, apart from an e-mail telling her she was a legend.

This tore at Jena's heart to the point where she took the risk of telling him she felt a little disappointed in his lack of appreciation. His reply was quite defensive. He basically said thanks, good luck, and take care. An overwhelming sensation of hurt and emptiness engulfed her, as he seemed uncaring. He didn't appear to acknowledge that her self-respect and dignity took a harsh knock with such a blunt message.

How could Jerry seem so insensitive towards Jena after all she had just done for him? Did he realise how hurt she was, and was it really that easy for him to cut her off like that?

Jena resigned herself to believing that she was wrong about her feelings and promised herself she would never allow anyone to treat her like that again. She felt worthless and unwise. She felt like she was the laughing stock for believing in herself, and she would be very careful about who she would offer such help to again. Although she was very smart, she had never felt so dumb and mistrusting at that moment. How could she not see it coming when all of the signs had been there right under her nose? How could she believe herself when she had been so wrong? Why had Jerry never given her a chance? She believed she had shown him who she was as a person and given him the opportunity to see her values in action; however, that hadn't been enough.

Although apprehensive, she wasn't surprised that Jerry messaged her the very next day to express his sincere apologies. He felt he had been very wrong and acted totally out of line, so being the kind of girl Jena was, she reservedly but genuinely accepted his apology. Jena knew Jerry had insecurities and fear, and she knew the feelings he was expressing all too well. She, too, had been let down terribly in the past, and she knew what was like to not have anyone in her corner, which made it hard for Jerry to accept the kindness she offered.

If nothing else, Jena knew Jerry was not used to having someone care much about him, so his boundaries were steely protected. In his past when things got tough and life was complicated, Jerry always ran away, he hid under his bed out of fear of failure and fear of his own feelings. It was a safe place for him where not one could see his insecurity or sense his lack of confidence. As Jerry was an intensely private man with private thoughts, he found someone so open like Jena hard to accept, but he couldn't quite put his finger on the likeness he found in her. They had shared such intimacy that had felt real and sensational to both of them. They had not intended to bond, but the special connection they had developed was worth something.

They had bonded for a reason; however, at that stage, neither of them knew what that reason was. One thing Jena was certain of was the fact that her spirits lifted when she was around him. An understanding of each other was beginning to flourish, and boundaries were beginning to take definition. More and more, they began to share stories of themselves, their past, insecurities, fears, likes, and dislikes. This established a new level of trust, and Jerry began to really appreciate Jena's caring nature and personal characteristics.

As the months passed and Jerry's birthday came around, Jena carefully selected a birthday gift, leaving it wrapped up in his favourite colours for him to find in the morning. It was important for Jena to show Jerry he could trust her and that she would be there for him if he wanted her in his life. This choice was about her, not him. She always believed happiness was the best solution to any problem. She did believe in him and felt she could help him do the same. Being herself around him was a must to get to know him better and drag him out from under his bed and mask of insecurity.

CHAPTER 10

Visibly Mystifying

You are the sun for their moon, the power for their strength,
their choice for their freedom, their bravery for their courage,
their kindness for their caring, their food for their thought, and
their kin for their ship.

The raunchy, stimulating, yet soft pleasure found them wanting time to stand still. Being mystified and in awe of each other's presence, they began to explore and visualise their desire and luring warmth as their bodies naturally entwined. Jena found herself in a curious new place of losing her inhibitions. Jerry licked and nibbled on her nipple while he tenderly grasped her breast. She could feel how hard he was with his erection pulsating against her inside leg. He teased with his tongue and kissed with his lips, and he knew that he wanted to pleasure every part of her body with every part of his. The thought of entering her became intense, but he enjoyed the anticipation and suspense, knowing

Man in the Mirror

Come my own way and ill not have a plan
I'll walk my own journey I'll be my own man
The world that I see will mean nothing to me
As I walk my own journey to my history

The people that come and the people that go
The end date is here before we all know
To see those who live who have no one around
A deaths all we see it's like no other sight to me

To sit and to watch as they take him away
A spiritless man who has nowhere to stay
I see him drive off in the back of a car
The man looks at me like he's going so far away

The man in the flat with the spiritless cat
He sees us he hears us his red wilted hat
And no one will care when that man passes on
Like a book that's been written and forwarded on to me

And as I walk on I just can't understand
I think of my journey I think of my plan
I think of their needs and I worry like hell
I think of their future that no one can tell

And please don't let them see me fall to my knees
When I stumble like hurdles get caught in the trees
I stand to my feet as the cycle comes round
The person I see is like no other sight to me

I sit and I think and I give up the drink
The man in the mirror is facing the brink
I look and I stare and I'm trying to see
What the man in the mirror is thinking of me

—Douglas Paterson, *Sycamore Road* 2011

his erection would finally lead him to where he wanted to be.

———~~~•◦◯◉◯◉◯◦•~~~———

As time passed, Jena put her own feelings aside. She felt Jerry needed encouragement, support, understanding, and care from another person. She had begun to see the person Jerry was—reluctant to love, hesitant to share his thoughts, anxious about change, fear of feelings. He led a visibly private life. Looking at himself, the man in the mirror in a soulful way was incredibly hard for him, as he would retreat within himself. He had come to depend only on himself for any support. Although he had a house to live in, his heart and soul were empty and homeless.

Jena wanted him to see that another human being could and would care about him. She wanted Jerry to see and feel loved for who he was and to realise there was no expectations from her, as he had enough expectations from his ex-wife. Jerry's mental space and emotional capacity were overloaded, and he was giving all he had without appreciation or recognition. He felt exhaustion from the demands and expectations his ex-wife placed on him. All Jena could do was let him know she was there for him if he needed her, although she knew because of his pride and male place in society, he would be incredibly reluctant to ask for anyone's help.

However apparent his mystifying ways were to Jena, she still felt there were reasons behind his mysterious eyes, and she had a desire to find out what made Jerry tick.

Why at times would he be with her and yet disappear and drift away while they were together?

Jerry had taught Jena invaluable lessons in life as a single person. He made her take notice of her own barriers as well as recognise her own strengths. He taught her to be herself without fear of retribution, which was a priceless lesson to Jena. Whether he had intended to teach her or not, he had no idea of the lessons Jena was learning from him. However, it was becoming increasingly obvious that Jerry would avoid and digress whenever Jena would become curious. This enigmatic approach appeared to be his protective shell. Jerry would either avoid answering or retreat into silence. *What is he so fearful of?* Jena wondered. It seemed he wanted to remain anonymous about himself and his life, even to a girl to whom he had disclosed many things that he had never told anyone.

Jena had seen a side to Jerry very few had—warm, loving, funny character with a mesmerising, magnetic charisma and a heart of gold, a man full of love to give that had been suppressed because of conditioning. Jerry was a man who had grown up in middle-class society and had been encouraged from a young age to not talk about his feelings or disclose problems and dare not cry. His steely resolve had seen him do what he was told, live by other's demands and expectations, and forget the song in his own heart. Men were certainly not allowed to give in to their fears or listen to their hearts because this could depict them as weak and soft. What was evident to Jena was that although Jerry was outwardly manly and physically strong, his inner strength of character was more admirable and valuable than anything else. This was clearly visible with the arrival of a new love, Maverick, his cat. Jerry was incredibly affectionate with Maverick and the bond they shared. His home and heart was no longer empty and closed off.

While Jena showed him what love, support, appreciation, kindness, and giving was like and gave Jerry a sense of calm, he still withdrew and drifted in and out. She felt if Jerry could feel comfortable reaching out to her, it would give him a sense of confidence and self-belief, which was missing in his life. Jena also felt this sense of calm around him as being with him also gave her a sense of happiness.

So as Jena and Jerry became closer as people, both of them couldn't put a finger on what exactly made them happy when they were with each other. They just felt it. They shared stories about their pasts, their families, and their friends. Neither of them had experienced this level of unity. There was an incredible physical and emotional attraction. The affection towards each other was at times electric. It was something that they couldn't explain. It was just a magic vibe and intense feeling. This attraction was more than their common interests like their love of books, movies, sports, food, and people watching. It was something that existed between two people. The fun was enticing and teasing, tempting and intimately, erotic yet frighteningly startling at times.

For Jena, every time Jerry physically touched her, a spine-tingling feeling would ignite inside of her. She knew she had to contain it, and she tried hard to keep a maintainable distance from Jerry. It was incredibly hard, considering she knew how she felt about him.

After a great night spent together laughing and sharing many intimate stories, Jerry reached out to give Jena a hug and kiss goodbye. Jena's spine-tingling feeling overcame her, and she indicated to Jerry that she wasn't keen to leave just yet. What came next was complete and utter heartbreak and confusion.

Jerry politely yet firmly rejected Jena's suggestion that she stay a little longer so that they could share a passionate moment like they had done in the past. He told her not to think there was any reason behind his refusal, and he simply said, "Not tonight." Jena was speechless and confused. She tried to hide her devastation and rejection as she picked up her dignity and self-respect along with her handbag and keys and then left.

As always Jerry walked her to her car, but she felt incredibly awkward and just wanted to leave immediately. She was so embarrassed, and she felt foolish for putting herself out there. After all, she was incredibly vulnerable to rejection.

Rejection shouldn't mean you aren't good enough for someone. Instead it, should mean that the other person failed *to see the beauty in you and what you have to offer them*, she thought.

Jena had never felt so alone. She knew that men loved sex and that if they rejected the offer of sex, it was either because they lacked complete interest and had no attraction in the girl or they were physically or emotionally unable to perform. Although Jerry had told Jena not to think about why he had refused her, her own self-awareness struggled to understand. Had she lost all sex appeal? Had she never had it? Had she lost her inner feminine beauty and charm? Had Jerry lost respect for her as a woman? Had Jerry lied to her, and had he never actually been interested in her? What the hell had happened? She thought to herself as tears streamed her face and that empty feeling engulfed her insides. She wasn't good enough or worthy enough to be loved. Simple.

The questions consumed her, and they dealt an enormous blow to her self-esteem. Were there other women? Was this his way of trying to push her out of his life for good because she was getting too close? In the end, there were no answers. From that night on, they never experienced another passionate moment. Jena could not face another blunt rejection like that. She had put herself, her dignity, and her vulnerability on the line only to fall flat, and she now felt like she had been hit head-on by a speeding train. Her own fears were now her reality.

In time, Jena accepted that Jerry had failed to see what he could have had with her. He was unable to accept her love, kindness, generosity, or friendship. She was incredibly hurt. She felt that raw, stabbing feeling in her throat. She felt she had let her own guard down and had tried hard to help Jerry overcome his own fears and lack of self-confidence. She had never wanted to change him, as she loved him as a person. She had only wanted to become a part of his life. Jena had to completely let the possibility go, and she had to see this for what it was—rejection. She felt she had to give up her feelings and dreams. *Giving up isn't losing. Giving in is.*

Jena had to face it. She had been dumped for no reason. Jerry was too polite to tell her she wasn't good enough. He had never taken her out. He had never followed through on his promises of a movie or a drink or anything else. She had to accept it. She was just an ordinary girl undeserving of happiness with another person.

With her self-esteem at an all-time low, she picked up her courage and dignity and maintained her distance from Jerry. She had to use every ounce of energy she had; she missed him so much. Once again, time away from the hurt would heal the wounds and help her pull herself back to reality as she knew it.

With the distance between them firmly in place, no reasons or answers about why this had happened, and a shattered heart beginning to heal, Jena began to get her life on track again. Many loved her still, and she knew it was Jerry's loss that he didn't want her in his life. Her confidence began to grow once again with the support of Sam and Marcus. Jena knew she would be okay.

At a time when all was going well for her, she received an e-mail, from none other than Jerry. *Why?* She thought to herself. Had he not caused her enough hurt, and had he not realised it was his choice to reject her? Why would he contact her again?

She read the e-mail, which said that his managers had highly commended his work report, which Jena had helped him with, and that he had been offered a promotion. He went on to say that he never would have gained such accolades if it hadn't been for her. He expressed his appreciation and gratitude in such kind words; however, Jena was well aware that he could be kind with his compliments. Jerry had told her in text messages and online chat before that he had appreciated her, but she knew he was only able to write it, not show it. With this appreciation, Jerry offered to take her out

The Place to Be

What can I do, what can I say?
Where is the meaning, behind all the fray?
Heading in the direction of hope,
Here I stand, and here I cope.

Like faith to the believer,
Can anyone see her?
Knowing she's there,
I just can't leave her.

Pulling aside, pushing some more,
A fresh breath of air I take with a grin.
Grab her back before she is gone.
Grasp her hand, her heart, and her kin.

Only I can take her where she's going.
It's me who knows the place to be.
All sparkling and glowing and delightful to see,
It's just like her, right inside of me.

There's no battle, no war to be lost or won,
For nothing much more can be done.
Encompassed by thoughts by kindness and truth,
Like pride and glory, we're together as one.

for a drink to celebrate and show her the appreciation she deserved for everything she had done for him.

The words "You're a legend" Jerry made Jena feel more foolish. The e-mail made Jena wonder, *Why did Jerry want to share his good news with me after rejecting me?* Jena could not bring herself to tell him how she felt, as she feared he would close off completely. Nor did she want to spoil his moment of great news. Although she was hurt, she was not the type to hurt him in any way or confront him about his broken promises. He was a fragile man and had suffered so much hurt in his life. The last thing Jena wanted to do was make him aware of her hurt feelings. She knew him well enough to know he would take on guilty feelings.

So Jena made her own choice to accept Jerry as he was. After all, he was the man she liked, not what he did or didn't do. She allowed the offer of a celebration drink to thank her be just that, an offer, and in that, the offer would probably never come to fruition. His offer was his way of saying thank you, but her cautious mind knew deep down he would never set a time or date.

Perhaps Jerry was just a procrastinator and was waiting for the right time; however, over a year had passed since the offer of the movies had come up. Plus, the recent rejection made Jena aware and mindful of reality.

Patience and understanding was what she needed. Pressure and expectation was the last thing Jerry needed, although Jena wished he wouldn't offer meeting if he knew he had no intention of following through with promises and invites. It hurt her purely because she really didn't have any answers why Jerry had rejected her, and yet he still felt comfortable contacting her.

Jena did not want to burden Jerry or remind him of the other offers he had made. All she wanted was for Jerry to feel happy and alive again. She knew she wanted him to smile, relax, and enjoy life, whether she was in it or not. His inner happiness was due to shine, and Jena had contributed to this. She hoped she had shown him how to love again. It was not about her happiness. It was about his. It was his choice to not give her a chance. Whether it was his lack of interest or a lack of his own self-belief that brought him to reject her, that no longer mattered. She had to go on living her life her way and protect herself from any potential broken promises made by anyone who would disappoint her. Perhaps disengaging her feelings and retreating was a lesson she had learnt from Jerry.

CHAPTER 11

Taking Chances

Just because someone says no once, twice, or a thousand times, that doesn't mean he or she will never say yes at the right time and place to the right person for the right reasons.

With sexual arousal and soft sensual touching, Jerry moved slowly down closer to that place to taste Jena's warm, wet, sweet femininity, influencing what was about to happen between them. Jena felt so shy before his eyes, but she wanted to feel the tip of his penis stroke her most inhibited place of ultimate pleasure. Jerry could no longer hold himself from craving the entry. In a swift yet utterly captivating movement, with Jena being so moist, he slipped the hard pulsating tender tip of his penis into a place of ecstasy. The moment of entry found them both in a euphoric state of pleasure.

After Jena received Jerry's e-mail, she decided it was worth taking a chance. After all, he could have ignored her, knowing she had not taken his rejection lightly. He knew he had hurt her feelings, but something had told him that he still wanted her in his life. She gave him credit for trying and taking a chance with her. She could have told him to never contact her again and forget about her.

With that in mind, Jena gave Jerry a chance to redeem himself and to see if he would follow up on the promise of a celebratory drink. On occasions, Jena would try to persuade Jerry to join her on outings. She knew how hard it was for him to leave his comfort zone. She offered many fun invites ranging from concerts to day trips with friends to just drinks. She also invited him to join her and her friends for birthday drinks. Nothing. Zero. Not even a card posted in the mail, just an informal yet warm text message first thing in the morning. The words were loving and delightful, but they were just words. The fact that he didn't want to see her on her special day made her protect her heart with a suit of armour. Jena couldn't understand this distance and detachment. She tried, which was all she could do. Absolutely nothing worked to get Jerry out. If she did get a response, he would just politely refuse, or he would just ignore her offers.

Jena's mind flowed with thoughts and questions. She had met him on the Internet. God, how stupid of her to think there was anyone from the Internet who had wanted her. The stories she'd heard were just about sex and nothing more, except a quick bit of fun while on a destructive emotional path and roller-coaster ride of self-denial. Men want a woman's body and passion as well as her ability to give and take for their own self-gratification. Or could it be that she saw or wanted to see in Jerry what he didn't see in himself?

She knew she could easily pick the ones who were smut talkers, the men who were so brash and upfront about sex. It's the ones with the charm and kind words that she knew all so well.

The night she had met Jerry, she felt that her search was over. She had found this amazing person inside a fearful but confident, charismatic, challenged, incredible, wholesome, hurt, damaged, beautiful soul. All she ever wanted was to find somebody to love … just a reflection of the famous song 'Somebody to Love' sung by the late Freddie Mercury of British rock group Queen. But all it seemed like was somebody to bed, nothing more, nothing less. It was all about sex and the suburbs.

To protect her own self-belief, she told herself if sex and the suburbs was on offer, then that is what she would also seek—just somebody to touch. The craving and sensual feeling of human touch, skin on skin, was too tempting for her to say what she truly wanted. It was just too hard to express, nothing but smut and humour to have her craving and desires met.

With her untouchable fantasies and her past hurt and pain, she could do nothing but accept what was available to her. And that was all okay with her. Having sex with someone gave her the ability to touch the one thing she wanted—but not the ability to feel it. To feel again was her ultimate desire because her numbness was becoming all too familiar.

How could she let down that barrier of numbness? What was the button that needed to be pushed? She didn't understand what it was or where it was. She just knew it needed a gentle nudge to feel excited, aroused, feminine, and euphoric. But what was the love she seemed to long for? Where did this come from? She had so many people who loved her, and she loved so many, but she had no one to be in love with.

That was the button. It was the one thing she lacked and the one thing she wanted. Everything else would fall into to place if someone would let her fall in love "with" him, not just allow her to love him. As most others thought since the beginning of time, with love comes sex, but she also knew relationships brought a whole lot more. Had she evolved before her time? Had it always been like this? Did men need sex to feel love and women need love to have sex? Was that the problem? What about the human traits developed by the human brain, such as understanding, respect, fun, communication, support, excitement, hugs, kisses, massages, protection, self-commitment? The list quite endless. Did they want next of kin, a person to dine with, to laugh with, to travel with, to live with, to argue with, to fight with, to grow old with, to learn with, to care for, to cook with, to clean with, to garden with, to just dance naked under the stars with?

It seemed no one wanted that anymore. In fact, had anyone ever wanted that? Was it a primal thing inside everyone to just have sex and never cohabitate? Was it human and social conditioning developed over the ages trying to mess with Mother Nature and dictate how men and women live in this world? Have we been conditioned to do as we should and need rather than do as we wish and want? Who had said it was wrong for us to just have human sex, chase our desires, and grab those untouchable fantasies when we can. However, the argument between her head and her heart remained challenging for Jena. If men and women were purely on this earth to reproduce and cohabitate, where did the act of cunnilingus and licking and sucking a penis come from? Pleasure or pornography?

Why did men seem to love to lick a woman's clitoris until she reached orgasm? Surely not the act of reproduction. And what about the act of a woman sucking a man's penis until he ejaculated? Was this the game of untouchable fantasy where the inhibitions of the mind, body, and soul came together? She could not understand why it was okay for men to openly talk about such acts and behaviour but if woman discussed these acts, it was vulgar and slutty. It was desire and seduction of the two sexes wanting and needing pure pleasure.

So why was she so attracted to Jerry as she recalled seeing him that first night? He didn't want anything she had to offer but friendship. He tried so hard to keep her at arm's length until she could no longer deny her attraction to him, wanting pure pleasure. It all started with a kiss. Why did men and women find a great kiss an automatic entry into one another? However, that only happened if the sensation was felt by both. Was this the beginning of human pleasure the kiss? She knew with his kiss, she would feel instant desire to touch the untouchable fantasy. The button had been nudged. She knew he could not hide his similar feelings through his vibe and totally exposed demeanour and character. However, she sensed Jerry was too afraid he would fuck up again.

Jena could not blame him, as no one wanted to fuck up again, especially when it came to relationships. Why would we want to experience hurt and turmoil and distress and tears? Why would we want to go through the loss and grief again? She felt that seeing someone was better than being alone. Her belief was this risk was better than going single to weddings, parties, funerals, journeys, and outings. And she felt all the hurt and distress could be avoided with the right person, the person with the same or similar values, the person who wants and not doesn't need to be there, the person who gets you when you're smiling, when you're laughing, when you're crying, when you're sick, when you're up, when you're down. She had sensed this was Jerry.

She felt all the people who had said being single was good were just liars because they hadn't found the right ones. Nor had they found themselves. Nor could they deal with headaches and issues that living and loving threw at us. They were living dead lives and existing instead of experiencing life with all its wonder. People like Jerry were missing out on the wonders of sharing, caring, giving, kindness, and all these had to offer.

Jena could see people were choosing to live in denial instead of grabbing an opportunity right in front of them. She had decided to choose happiness and love over anger and resentment. She wanted to have a life where good and bad was made easier with a shoulder to cry on, a hand to hold, an ear to listen, a body to hug, lips to kiss, a hand to scratch where you couldn't reach. She knew this was what you had when you were not single.

She wanted a path to travel with someone to share, someone to walk beside her.

When she had met Jerry, she found she had picked one who did not want to share her path, someone who didn't know how to create his own purely because he lacked self-belief. Lacking this had held him prisoner of his own secret battle. He had convinced himself and others that he was doing it his way. However, he didn't even know what his way actually was.

For Jerry, he knew he craved human touch; however, he denied himself it. He knew he wanted it but believed he couldn't have it. Jena suspected that either infidelity had screwed him up or he felt he had just simply chosen the wrong one. But the only way to find the right one was to take a risk, take a chance, believe, and know what you wanted. True happiness came from within. You needed self-belief and the ability to recognise that "happiness is not getting what you want but wanting what you have already." Jerry didn't recognise or acknowledge what he wanted and what he had in Jena. She felt he had her hook, line, and sinker, yet he wanted to keep her on the hook and not enjoy the many benefits she could bring to his life.

When she offered him kindness, it created a lump in his throat. He found it incredibly hard to keep those feelings inside, yet his barrier to deny himself what he truly wanted held him back. She gave him what she thought he needed—affection, attention, and tender, loving care. It was not a tangible or material gift of his favourite aftershave or the book he would enjoy. She listened to his body language and his outward behaviour towards her and took notice of his delightful vibe. He seemed so lost and so let down by others who had not given him any of this for a long time. Others had blamed him for the way he was, fostering less and less self-belief.

Jena couldn't work out why others had hurt this beautiful soul. Why had he felt so low that he had to leave situations to save himself? How had he gotten to a stage in his life where he wanted to move forward yet didn't know how to? Is it addiction perhaps or more an addictive personality?

In the beginning, Jena suspected he only wanted her for sex and naughtiness, her cheeky sense of humour, and her genuine friendship, yet now he had realised that he wanted more. This kept her coming back without any need, merely want.

She adored him yet abhorred herself for loving his qualities, his charm, his soul, his cheekiness, his uniqueness, his touch, his kiss. She knew it was his kiss that sold her. It kept her loathing of her own feelings yet incredibly wanting of his love. So she began to search for the answers to her questions.

Jena took many chances at the risk of ignorance and refusal. However, she was a girl who was willing to take chances, hoping she may just make someone happy. When she looked at Jerry objectively, she saw a man who feared his own happiness, and she wanted him to see that life was full of opportunity. With her offers and invites, she just wanted to give him the opportunity to see there was much more to life than his past, his work, and his own comfort zone.

Because she was brutally honest, incredibly forthright, but also nurturing with a healthy respect for fear, her attitude was inspiring and positive. She had her own insecurities about love and life, and she had overcome adversity many times. She had developed her own steely resolve, looking at opportunity as nothing to lose and everything to gain. Her belief was that life was a chance worth taking; it was not a rehearsal. Unless we had first lost, we had no idea how to win, and the only way to win was to take chances in life, as Jena had learned by not giving up on Jerry.

Jena's knowledge and experiences in building resilience in her own life gave her the courage to help others do the same. The intimacy she and Jerry shared had become a distant memory; she believed he needed a constant in his life, a person who cared about his well-being, something he had been lacking for many years.

Therefore, every time she saw Jerry, she took the chance to show him what consistency in caring meant to her and allow him to open up. Honesty was the most consistent thing she showed him. Her commitment to being there and showing him that he did matter saw Jerry continue on his life path with nothing much changing. His Ground Hog Days turned into weeks and then into months, and although he spoke about changing many things in his life, so many things remained the same.

Jerry seemed to lack not just confidence but also motivation. This brought Jena to the realisation that Jerry was silently suffering from a form of depression. Jena knew the signs and symptoms, as she was involved in identifying depressive symptoms with her clients from work. It was an extremely touchy subject to address. Because Jerry chose

The Empty Corner

I look around in a crowded room.
I see a range of colours in bloom.
I see the many faces looking at me,
But I am lost in a crowded sea.

The bystanders they stare,
And some of them glare.
They're all on the sidelines,
And my corner is bare.

I'm looking for you.
You're looking too.
I see a light.
It's your face, so bright.

Maybe I'm amazed
When I see your gaze.
The sidelines are clear.
I have nothing to fear.

As I turn around
And look behind,
But there is nothing to see
Behind beautiful me.

That's when I realise
I must turn the tide.
The corner is empty
Because you're right by my side.

the quiet and private life, very few saw this side of him; however, Jena saw so much potential for him to shine. It appeared like keeping Jena at arm's length was the only way Jerry could get to know and trust her. He had lived so long on his own that keeping people at arm's length had become his way of life.

Jerry was such an intelligent man with so much to offer. She was hopeful one day he would see this and take a chance and find something or someone who would inspire him. He certainly wasn't apprehensive about asking Jena questions about her life. Nor was he anxious about pleasing her in their intimate moments. The most frustrating part of this endeavour was finding the way to get him there.

This reluctance of Jerry made Jena feel alone in her own corner. In her adult life, she had become accustomed to the feeling of having no one to back her up.

This was a feeling Jerry was also very used to. He, too, had always felt his corner was empty, yet both Jerry and Jena felt they were the first ones to step into others' corners to please them and not themselves. Their similarities were uncanny. They both wanted to "keep others happy."

CHAPTER 12

Keeping Others Happy

I always feel a bit like an outsider, but it is what it is.

Grabbing hold of his self-control to avoid an instant orgasm, Jerry indulged in pleasuring Jena with thrusting himself up against her to reach deep into a place of paradise. He hadn't felt or connected like this with a woman in a long time, and the passion she expressed found him wanting so much more time, so much more sensational time. Jena's seduction was in her body language and her vibe. She giggled in harmony with his thrusts. The pure delight was bliss and edgy, such a naughty experience mixed with a sense of tender, loving care.

———◦◦◦◦◦———

Over time, Jerry realised he could depend on Jena. She seemed like one who would not walk away easily or give up on people. She believed in people and showed enormous respect for others' choices. She, too, kept people at arm's length at times; however, she made an effort to keep good people in her life. Jerry realised Jena was everything she had said she was. She kept to her word and honoured her own values of love, respect, honesty, and integrity. Her will appeared incredibly strong, and her passion was intimately suggestive with a warm, sincere, vibrant affection about her.

Jerry had found someone he could trust and to whom he could open up (even if it was ever-so-slightly). He felt very comfortable knowing he could talk to her. She would listen to him, help him, support and encourage him, and be there for him. Jerry felt so lucky, but he knew his distance. His heart felt like it had been touched for the first time in a long time, though he struggled so much to show it and couldn't bring himself to let Jena into his life. Something was stopping him, yet he couldn't tell her what it really was.

Jerry had only told a couple of his friends about Jena on a drunken night out. Jena asked herself if she was just a bragging notch in his belt or someone he spoke highly of and wanted to hang on to. His family knew nothing of her, yet Jena knew she had made a positive impact in his life. Why would he not tell others about her and what she had done for him? Although Jerry reassured Jena that every part of him truly appreciated her, he wouldn't take a chance on loving her. His emotional resilience had been damaged and rocked to its core by his past. Jerry really didn't know if he could allow himself to love again. What Jerry didn't realise was that Jena was extremely cautious herself to the point of not allowing anyone into her own heart. She would give all the love she had to others but not allow anyone into her own sacred place. To a great extent she wanted him to know that she would never hurt him intentionally and would rather walk away than either face hurt or disappointment. Although there was something so very different about Jerry that she felt naturally drawn to, however she still felt almost relief that he didn't want her. She was off the hook because he rejected her so she would not have to let down her own guard there was no way anyone was going to get close enough to her. On the outside she portrayed love, understanding, compassion and consideration though she found it almost impossible to allow someone to love her. To love unconditionally was easy but to be loved by another unconditionally was something she felt she couldn't accept. She wasn't good enough and time and time again men had proven that to her so she had learned to live with that for such a long time it became part of her nature. Jerry's rejection was a proof and cemented this belief inside her. She knew she was loved by others and she gave love unconditionally she was unlovable.

So as sensitive as they both seemed they continued to stay in contact on a "friends" basis. As they now began to really open up, Jena became a lot more aware of how much Jerry's ex-wife had abused his trust and the high expectations and guilt she had targeted him with. Jerry took in a very good income, but he was living like a pauper, eating two-minute noodles, TV dinners, and jam sandwiches. He had very little money to survive on, barely enough to keep a roof over his head and food in his stomach. He didn't realise Jena was in a similar position;

For Jerry

That Spark

When I said goodbye that night, my spark turned into fun.
The hope I felt knew that you could be the one.
As cheeky banter, care, and trust carried through the weeks,
My mind and heart began to heal the holes and all the leaks.

Then one day, I don't know when, the contact all but stopped.
My thoughts they waned but did not go. I felt I was dropped.

I carried on my daily life with you not far from thought.
I went about my single life without you in my court.
My memory had all but lost the very thought of you,
Yet that lovely click, that little spark ignited right out the blue.

That one fine day, my phone it chimed, a message brought to light.
You, too, had felt that magic spark, which we had shone so bright.
You had wondered with tempting delight what happened to that girl,
The one you liked and shared a moment, as close as oyster and pearl.

I wondered why we were so shy, yet bonded all so well,
So from then on, I took a chance to see if you could tell.

As time passed, I began to grow an open, trusting mind
To find if you would take me as the warm and tender kind.
You finally offered that lovely date, where we met beside the sea.
Excitement beckoned when we met again, just us, just you
and me.

We laughed and smiled, talked, and walked, yet cautious I
would be,
But something told me deep inside that both of us could see.
I knew my wall it had built up, protecting my fragile heart,
Though something pulled it down a little, even when we were
apart.

You did not run or walk away from what you felt was right,
Though I knew I must find a friend, firstly to gain insight.

I kept my distance, knowing my fear would be showing.
I did not want to jump ahead or end up back in bed.
I stayed well back and guarded in my corner all alone
But found myself drawing near, where the seeds were being
sown.

The days and nights were shared by words all warm and
caring.
I began to wonder how much of me was worth all the sharing.
I let go a piece of me no man had ever seen.
I gave to you a secret, where you would see me beam.

That warm night we shared a drink, that spark again it rose,
Unlike the flower, no thorn in sight, just your scent to guide
my nose.
Something that night changed me to be the woman whom you
saw,
My intimate charm and cheekiest smile, all glowing from my core.

A friendship had formed, one that welcomed care.
At that time all I wanted was to see how much you'd share.
I was fearful then of the fact you may not want just me,
But I let go that piece of me to see what was to be.

I was happy to give you that, but somehow, I felt I knew
That potentially and possibly, I could be the one for you.
I wanted you to see the beauty inside of me,
To unlock my love inside my heart, and for you to hold the key.

Out of the blue, you said to me, it wasn't me but you.
All along I felt it wasn't you but me; I knew this to be true.
You said you had to find the answers you did not quite yet
know.
I wish I could have told you then that I should have let you go.

I unwrapped my little finger from the secret I gave to you
To move on back to my own life, to give you freedom too.
I tried so hard to let you go, yet something drew me back,
Knowing that that click, that spark, had gone from white to black.

I realised something missing; I had to find out what.
My phone it chimed, and you again, that something was a lot.

I jumped back in to help you find the future with hopes and
dreams.
This time round, I was too proud, too strong, or so it seems.
We grew and learnt together, where we couldn't run and hide.
What I saw and what I found was me right by your side.

Although arm's length, there we were, sharing our time between
Our laughs, our secrets, our hopes and dreams, like never
before we'd seen.

I cared. I gave a gift from all I had.
I felt I must open up, a touch of me, a tad.
From all the times you said no, I trusted you were shy.
I set out to find out what, the very reasons why.

I found out a lovely man had hurt and often ran.
So I came to you to give you hope as I know I can.
I never planned to fall in love, just seek a common bond.
I was just as scared as you, yet I grew very fond.

I never sought a lover, just a friend to say hello,
But I found a kindred soul. I didn't want to let go.
To someone I did like, I invested my time and heart.
I feel I found a man unknown where I never want to part.

The time has come for me to say,
To risk losing you today.
My words are not empty, not scary or wrong.
Nothing has felt more right, and I've known it all along.

All I want to do is spend some time with you.
If you're not ready, not willing or sure, I promise I'll go too.
I can truly say that I do love someone who taught me much,
Something beyond my words and meaning, simply beauty in
your touch.
That spark, it's real, and what I feel I hope you know by now.
What's for us will not go past us. Jerry, please take a bow.

however, Jena was fortunate enough to have good people help her out.

Because she owned her own business, she also had a lot of allies and contacts. From time to time, she did consulting work for them, either earning goods in kind or vouchers for places she could not afford to go. On one occasion, she was given a new washing machine and LCD TV. Being the kind of girl Jena was, she decided to give Jerry the LCD TV. He had dreamt of owning one but could never afford to buy one. To Jena, it was not a material item that couldn't buy happiness or satisfaction, nor was there an option to sell it, as it wasn't worth the hassle for her to organise doing so. She had too many priorities in her life, including keeping her business afloat and reorganising her own life.

It wasn't a matter of if or when. It was a matter of how. Jena had a courier deliver it to Jerry's house. She knew it was possible that he would refuse her generosity; however, she was not about to take no for an answer. She believed everyone deserved a little pleasure in their lives, and Jerry had sacrificed his own pleasures to keep others happy. However, Jena's core beliefs were about giving to give, not giving to receive. All she wanted from Jerry was for him to notice her and give her a chance to show him who she was and to accept her heart into his.

Although Jerry and Jena had occasionally shared a bottle of wine at his place, they had never been out since they had gone on that coffee date. Jerry had promised many times that he would take her out; however, his pride and lack of money were always on his mind. Jerry really wanted to give something nice and do something nice for

Jena; however, he never told her, and he didn't know that Jena didn't want anything but his time.

So as Jerry continued to keep others happy, he left Jena out of his social life and family life. Jerry was cautious and struggled to express his feelings for her, although he knew there was a spark between them. Jena herself didn't want to jeopardise the warm relationship they had built as friends. She loved him with all her heart, yet his behaviours somewhat perplexed her. She did not want him to change in any way. He was still the man she had initially been attracted to. Acceptance was all about being together as they were, no expectations of the other; however, a strong attachment kept them liking each other. Their friendship was caring and courageous, yet the distance Jerry created caused Jena to feel that he didn't feel much for her at times, although his words and the chemistry and spark between them when they were together told Jena otherwise.

CHAPTER 13

That One Thing

One smile can take away one thousand tears.

Jena sensed Jerry was hungry for more. An urge came over her to hug him close to her body, and he pushed his way through his fearful emotions. His body was telling her he wanted to pause time, yet the vibe of his physical connection was not what appeared to be hungry for. It was more than touch. It was intimacy and feeling. He was numb, and he feared the intensity that he was engaging in with Jena. The harder he thrust his pelvis, the more vigorous he became. He was almost lost in that moment of entry. As their bodies trembled, Jena clung to his shoulders and wrapped herself against the naked hunger of his desires.

Jerry was a lover of movies, particularly comedy—dark comedies, the light–hearted kinds, and even romantic comedies.

Jerry loved to laugh, but he loved to make others laugh even more. This was his way of giving and connecting. This was what he gave to Jena. The missed drinks, broken promises, the lack of movie nights, and the lack of invites for drinks mattered to Jena, but him making her laugh and smile was the best feeling in the world.

He had a fabulous wit about him. He was able to turn heads with his funny comments and natural light–hearted fun. Wherever he went, he would create a fun environment, even at work, where the moral police would keep an eye on his behaviour. Although this dampened his spirit, his enthusiasm, and his love of laughing, this never stopped his warm and funny personality from shining. Comedy was Jerry's stage, his natural habitat.

It wasn't the jokes he told or the words he used. It was Jerry's ability to express them in a meaningful, light–hearted, loveable manner. His style, grace, and affection was what made him shine. Unfortunately, this secret was something Jerry couldn't see or believe he even had. Jena had seen this from the moment she met him. This was his magic, his strength, his power, beyond any physical attraction to him that she had. This style, grace, and affection was how he aroused, tempted, flirted, and communicated with her. It was intimate, personal, open, and giving, and it turned on her mind, body, heart and soul.

Jena often found herself mesmerised by Jerry's attractive, magnetic style, which, when in his presence, drove her to cross her own personal boundaries. This eloquent affection tamed the girl many had known to be a little wild at heart. However, Jena adored this about Jerry, but she found it hard to tell him because of his disengaging and uncommitted manner. Jena knew she was able to maintain self-control most of the time, holding her barriers well up and her guardedness in place. The trouble was she found it extremely difficult and almost impossible at times to tell her mind to stop loving him when her heart still felt so strongly for him.

Jena, though, was very grateful that Jerry had told her that she had been the only woman with whom he had shared some of his insecurities. Whether in text, real life, or pillow talk, the instant attraction never waned for the reserved, naïve, but wild-hearted Jena.

She had never experienced this in her life before, and although she was a fiercely independent and capable woman, Jena realised that Jerry could melt her in a moment with his charismatic affection. He had the enormous capacity to make her weak at the knees, and he knew that he could draw her near and also keep her at arm's length any time he wanted. It was a powerful yet very seductive feature about him.

His kissing was affectionate. His hugging, although distant and reluctant at times, was heart-warming. His personality was charismatic, and his lovemaking with his hard, erect, pulsating penis was provocatively magnificent. Incredible feelings so engulfed Jena that words were impossible at times. It took her a while to work out that Jerry could have anything his heart desired from her if he used his affectionate nature; however, he was too frightened to use it.

The One Thing

Warm and tender,
Soft and smooth,
Luscious and lust,
A kiss a must.

With mystical magic,
A moment to live,
It comes from within
To share and to give.

The affection so rare,
The desire to touch,
An embrace not to miss,
Caressing, such bliss.

The one thing we know
When our heart is aglow
Is that spark, that flame,
And that smile we show.

It appears in our eyes
Just like the sun.
It's warm, and it's bright,
The purest of fun.

Under the surface
It's bursting to rise.
It blossoms like spring,
A tempting surprise.

A feeling it takes
Some time to see.
It springs from a place
The heart that is free.

People liked him, but his insecurity often made him feel that he was inadequate and unpopular. He found this hard to accept, and his awareness of his insecurity overpowered his confidence so much that it brought him to live his very private life in his home in the northern suburbs. Jena knew she could be intimately suggestive, drop hints, tempt and tease, but this would not lead to significance, value, or true meaning. She understood men more than Jerry realised. After all, she had grown up with brothers and a very unaffectionate father. Although her brothers were able to express themselves and knew the true meaning of love, they, too, found affection awkward just like Jerry.

However, she saw how much he oozed confidence when he would let his guard down. His humour was wittier, his confidence higher, his demeanour more relaxed, his heart more open and warm, and he shone brightly like the sun.

Jena felt so drawn to this side of him. It was the one thing she had never experienced from a man or herself. She was a girl who didn't need a big house, flashy cars, fashionable clothes, material items, or fancy things. She wanted a man to kiss her forehead and tell her how lucky he was to have her in his life. Money couldn't buy this affection. She didn't need marriage or another person to look after her. She just wanted this special someone, and to her, Jerry was that person. When she had that affection, everything was possible.

Jerry had "the one thing" in the palm of his hands, literally. He was the boy from the north, the man in the mirror, the gentleman within, with perfect hands to give and hold on to. Jerry represented the three colours of his beloved "Dogs"—red for passion, blue for bravery, and white for purity—yet he could not see this for himself. His arms were those of a man who could hold the strength of his will but also take the load off others' shoulders with ease. He struggled to do this for himself though. He filtered his love and emotion and gave himself to those who were distant from him because getting too close was too frightening for him. Someone knowing the real Jerry was distressing territory for him. To show and give affection was what he craved, but he couldn't find the person he was comfortable with until he met the engaging, affectionate, loveable, and genuine Miss Jena Jones.

Jena challenged Jerry at times with her remarkable sense of unconditional love and openness. Although Jerry lived alone with his beloved cat, he was aware of the world around him. Her memory was sharp and guided, and she seemed to have great insight and instinct like no girl he had met. She provoked not only his thoughts but also touched his heart with real feeling and emotion.

To Touch a Thought

A thought does not come from the brain.
It comes from the heart. It can heal any pain.
An inborn desire to think with our mind,
A thought is the link for us to be kind.

Imagine a place where thinking is pure.
Open your heart. You'll find it for sure.
To touch a thought is not done with a finger.
It's heartfelt affection and a pleasure to linger.

CHAPTER 14

Accurate Observation

Do we see with our eyes … or look with our hearts?

Each thrust of his was intense, and they soon began a fast orgasmic rhythm. He drove and focussed on his powerful senses through his pulsating hard penis and glowed in the visual splendour. He found himself mesmerised by Jena's feminine beauty, her perfumed scent and smiling face. She was a divine, flawless pleasure to fuck. She was presenting the urge to be bound by their flesh and passion for each other in the moment. Jerry touched Jena in places of virginity, stirring and captivating, releasing her inner shyness as she savoured and relished in liberating her sensuality.

Jerry liked to observe the world around him. He liked to read and learn from different experiences. Although observant, he would shy away from being reflective. He was reluctant to take steps to change some things because he knew how people often reacted. Some felt sorry for him and liked to include him, but he knew at times he just wouldn't fit in to other people's expectations. This was a strength he had within himself, as he had learnt from his past. Although he had a very relaxed attitude to the outside world, his feelings for others challenged him. His values and principles were wholesome, but other people's actions and behaviours would find him retreat and withdraw.

Living in a rut was what he believed he needed for a peaceful life. Like many "normal" people, he didn't like conflict. He saw how others acted, and he felt the impact. But he was a man of integrity, and some would say selfishness, as society had demanded too much from him and had led him to his lonely life. The pressure to perform at work and do a good job, keep his ex-wife happy in her comfortable lifestyle, give his daughter everything she wanted and needed, and keep his distance from his son because of his chosen partner stirred up unwanted anger inside him. He knew that wasn't healthy. He only had minimal contact with his dad because his dad's new wife had very different values and principles and lacked compassion for his circumstances and choices. Because of all this pressure, Jerry felt obliged to conform to everyone else and had very little time to enjoy his own life. He carried bitterness and anger inside his heart and couldn't bring himself to deal with it. Despite these pressures, though, Jerry found a very small amount of time to allow Jena into his life and his heart. For some unknown reason, he felt she was right, although he kept her at arm's length.

Jerry developed trust and a sense of security with Jena. He could truly be himself with her and realised it was okay and safe to allowing her to know him. She did not judge him, criticize him, or put pressure on him. She appeared to be a very respectful listener and appeared unfazed by Jerry's sometimes complicated yet organised life. She always managed to stay true to herself, and she supported and encouraged him to talk to her. She had an amazing bravery about her and constantly reassured him that talking about things would make him feel better. He told Jena how relaxed she made him feel and how she always managed to make him feel better about himself. However, Jena was very aware that at any given moment, he could retreat into his shell and close up.

But how much did Jerry know about Jena? She was also a girl who would close up and retreat into her shell. She would rather be an infinite wallflower than speak up about her feelings. Jerry knew Jena had a versatile and interesting career. She was divorced, and she had had a violent marriage and hostile separation. He knew she had children, who were her whole life. He knew she loved football and she was a very positive girl who loved to help others. She was also extremely loyal and loving with her friends and family. He knew she loved to laugh and share a good story and a good joke. She loved to smile and share the vibrancy of life. He knew she shared his love of reading, movies, and people-watching and loathed stupidity and ignorance. He knew she loved to share her thoughtfulness and generosity, her kindness and caring.

The Beginning of Me

You engage me, you encourage me,
You teach me, and more.
You feel me, you hold me,
You kiss me, I adore.

You seduce me, you arouse me,
You give me a smile.
You please me, you tease me,
You make it worthwhile.

You talk to me, you listen to me,
You surprise me with fun.
You get me, you enjoy me,
You are second to none.

You allow me, you squeeze me.
You care when I need,
You receive me, you believe me.
You fill me with creed.

You respect me, you support me,
You freed me from guise.
You open me, you excite me,
You are my first prize.

You warm me, you touch me,
You calm me no end.
You awaken me, you like me,
You call me your friend.

You tempt me, you delight me,
You entice me to see.
You found me, you charm me,
You are the beginning of me.

He knew how passionate, zealous, loving, sexy, sassy, delightful, and charming she was inside and outside the bedroom.

Jerry had told her how he wanted to change and to get out of his rut because he didn't want to reach retirement, look back on his life, and wish he had done more than work. Jena had told him that only he could decide his future, but she was happy to help and guide him. And although he knew that Jena had the ability to be calm him in difficult circumstances and that she would help him, he was still very reluctant to act on his thoughts. He was extremely wary on showing any affection or any signs that he was truly interested in her.

Jena knew if he really wanted her help and really wanted the change, he would take steps to do so. She couldn't do it for him, but fundamentally, she knew the nature and extent of her own knowledge plus her values. She had helped many people change their direction with time and patience, and she had contributed what she could. Jerry was no different.

But what did Jerry not know about Jena? Did he know she was extremely self-conscious and vulnerable? Did he know her level of effort and determination to succeed in her career? Did he know how really shy she was and how she used her outward confidence as a mask for how she felt about herself? Did he see that she wanted to touch people in a compassionate and understanding way? Did he know what her friends and family thought of her? Did he realise how much her heart was broken and damaged and how very protective she was of her feelings?

Although Jerry saw a confident, happy, open woman who talked and laughed a lot, she rarely spoke of herself. She spoke of what she knew and what she had learned and what her experience of life was but very very rarely spoke of her true self. He didn't realise that she struggled with discussing and expressing her hurt and pain because she was unable to express her feelings without tears. She didn't want anyone to see her tears because they were a sign of extreme vulnerability. It was this vulnerability she was frightened of the most because she felt wide open to abuse, rejection, and harm. She protected this with a smokescreen. She felt she could not compete with strong, beautiful women, and she would always retreat to being the infinite wallflower. Appearing confident was easy, and thoughtfulness and kindness were in her nature, so she used these strengths. She was a beautiful bed of roses behind a barbed wire fence. Jena still had a dynamic way of sharing because like Jerry, she was an accurate observer of the world around her. She had learnt to watch others, particularly those people she looked up to and admired. Jerry didn't realise he was adored and admired by her because she, too, was reluctant to share that part of herself. Jena often wondered what he observed in her and about her. What and who did he really see? But he was always happy to share kind words with her, which continually inspired Jena.

Jena began to feel she was blessed by having Jerry in her life. The one word that represented what she felt was love. She felt love had escaped her in the way he had offered it. She knew love from her children, family, and friends, but she didn't know love like the kind she had for Jerry.

It was cautious love, protected love, secured gold inside a vault. It was a curious love that continually surprised her, but the love she gave Jerry was unconditional and loyal because that was all she knew.

Jerry, though reluctant to admit it, had been impacted by Jena's love. It was unconditional without expectation. Jena always dared to be different from others. She put her heart on the line for love, and she wore it on her sleeve. Although at times she felt like the invisible wallflower, she knew she could make a difference by giving her love. She could share it, give it away, and not allow anyone to give her any in return.

Being the accurate observer and the invisible wallflower, she saw that many people seemed to have forgotten how to think. Sincerity had been replaced by consumerism. Love had been replaced with no-strings-attached sex, and thoughtfulness had been replaced with selfishness. Self-confidence had been replaced with narcissism. Seeing had been replaced with looking. Listening had been replaced with hearing. Sniffing was the new sense of smell. Eating was the new tasting experience, and a touch was no longer a feeling. It was a poke. Conflict was the new comfort, denial the new responsibility, and tears were for the weak. It appeared the word love in this generation was obsolete and people were immune to it. Love was no longer behavioural. It was simply another word.

However, Jerry and Jena, who were both in their forties, knew that this generation would not last. It appeared to both of them that this version of society was pulling further away from their own traditional values.

They were being sucked into the juggernaut of the current "now" society. Although people didn't want traditional values, they still craved to have what the Joneses had, including a family to love, a loyal partner, a nice house, a nice car, a good job, money in the bank, a flat-screen TV, an annual holiday, a home computer, a holiday house, a cliquey group of friends, youthful looks, a great sense of humour, no criminal record, support the most popular team, a great sex life, and true happiness. As well as a be a member of a club, well behaved children, a cool hobby, have hundreds of friends on social networking sites, a best friend, a white picket fence with all the bells and whistles, just like the Joneses. They wanted it all and wanted it now but were not prepared to do the hard work or face many of life's complications and complexities. Everyone wanted the easy life, and they didn't want to work hard for it. This kind of pressure was the reason both Jerry and Jena found themselves in divorce courts. The 'now' society was the reason there was highly conflicting home lives, children running amok, and friends taking sides.

People would rather poke a pen in their eyes than deal with a system of a smart world with stupid people. Mother Nature appeared to have bipolar disorder. Common sense had gone insane. Tourette's syndrome was the new excuse. "It's all about me" was the new fashion. "In a minute" took a whole day. Everything was epidemic. Control and demand were not negotiable. Manipulation and lies were the values of love. Simplicity had gotten lost in the hard drive of life.

However Jerry and Jena realised they weren't like the Joneses. They were individuals with their own separate identities in a fucked up world of lost souls and wrongdoings. This similarity gave them a sense of belonging with each other. Jerry really enjoyed his time with Jena; her company was refreshing and her individuality was welcoming.

CHAPTER 15

Gold in a Coalmine

Begin. Believe. Become.

With temptation and anticipation now far from their minds, Jerry and Jena reached the point of no return where the surge of orgasm saw them erupt simultaneously with intensity and intimate pleasure. Triggering inner ecstasy, spellbound by ecstatic bliss from the pulsating rhythm and penetration of his penis fully engulfed and grasped by her inner muscle spasms. Jerry had found the magic combination for her to experience the multiple orgasmic state of sexual stimulation with his both mind and body. He was a man who invested in her being and her pleasure. The tingling sensation erupted throughout her whole body and mind where Jerry had left an eroticized impression on her. He had tantalised her to crave so much more of the succulence and lusciousness of his attentiveness as she wanted to become a lot more

Pondering Eruptions

Your rudeness excites me.
It bites me.
It delights me.
Your smile it bends me.
It sends me.
It mends me.

Your lust and body,
A calming thing
Yet twitching and turning
With your other brain.
Oh, not a smile that reminds me of pain.

Your hardness of thinking,
A wet eruption a-plenty
With volcanic matter.
As the earthquake it shatters,
Your penis gets fuller and fatter.

My mind is wandering.
My cunny is pondering
The way that I remember
How nice it can be
With you erupting inside me.

How naughty, I say.
At the end of the day
It's a natural picture of pleasure and fun,
Just a nice soothing thought,
The orgasm you brought.

A guide to the words,
A hand to pull,
All of the come that sits inside
Coming out of the tube,
Only my words as lube.

To excite, to delight, to bite,
There's more
To come, and to some
The scene is set.
Here I come with a lick I get—

Dreaming of the Day

Sitting all alone, when everyone has been,
A little hint lights up inside, something that you've seen
Dreaming of the day, when all you have around
Is that other soul by your side, so happy that you found.

Nature and her mother are formed for you to know
That time and his father can't wait for you to glow,
Shining like the sun and beaming like the moon.
Don't wait for time or nature for your happiness to bloom.

familiar and aware of his sensual energy for sexual pleasure that she had experienced.

————⁓⁓◦◦◦◦◦◦◦⁓⁓————

Jerry slowed the distracted pace within moments and gently and delicately kissed the delightful Jena with a lingering sensitivity that made her whole body tingle with warmth and affection. Her body and senses captured the moment with rawness and vulnerability. She found herself no longer resisting the affection and attention she had received.

Though Jerry was still in an awe-like state and he was disengaged to his disposition of introversion, his safety mechanism button to exclude emotions and feelings was still switched to on. Jena had felt him become so close and intimate with her that she knew he just wouldn't allow himself to feel such magical feelings of desire. She could feel the bond they shared and how strong and right it was; however, his emotional numbness and past hurt would soon prevent him from sharing his heart with another.

Jerry Smith knew that someday, sometime he would be okay. He knew his life was better than most others, even if he felt that he was in a rut. He frequently felt challenged by others' expectations; however, he maintained his own values and his sense of style, and he knew class when he saw it.

The boy from the northern suburbs had settled in his comfort zone but was now beginning to see life outside of his lounge room. Jena had given him a new perspective on life. He knew he wanted to travel like others, but not alone. He wanted freedom with companionship and contentment. Jena too wanted the same thing.

Jerry reflected on the words his late grandfather Alexander, who had written to his grandmother almost 80 years ago. His grandfather was a coalminer and his grandmother was the sparkle of gold in his heart and mind where he spent so much of his life in the cold dark world, miles underground. She was his gold in a coalmine.

Jerry had found these letters in an old box that hadn't been touched for years. They were yellow and fragile and barely legible however he managed to interpret them.

6th August, 1939

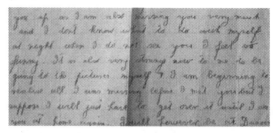

'you up as I am also missing you very much and I don't know what to do with myself as right when I do not see you I feel so funny. It is also very strange now to me to be going to the pictures myself and I am beginning to realise all I was missing before I met you but I suppose I will just have to get over it until I see you at home again. I will however be at . . .'

'before, if I know the way to where you are I might have to come for a day if I would just get a place to stay'

'from your sweet Alex to my lollipop' Eck

2nd May 1955

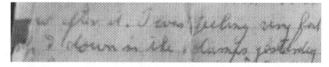

'in after it. I was feeling very fed up and down in the dumps yesterday'

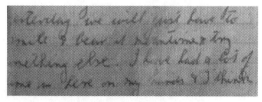

'yesterday we will just have to smile and bear it meantime and try something else. I have had a lot of time in here on my hands and I think'

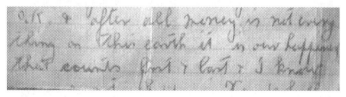

'O.K. and after all money is not everything on this earth it is our happiness that counts first and last and I know'

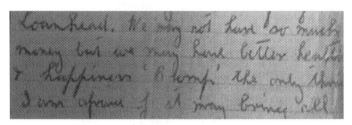

'Loanhead. We may not have much money but we may better help and happiness 'Bump' the only thing I am afraid of it may bring all'

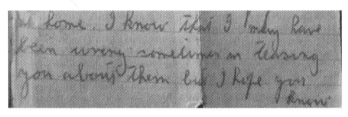

'at home. I know that I may have been wrong sometimes in teasing you about them but I hope you know'

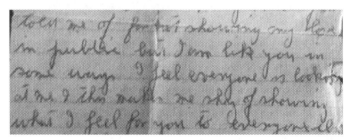

'told me off for not showing my love in public but I am like you in some ways I feel everyone is looking at me and this makes me shy of showing what I feel for you to everyone else'

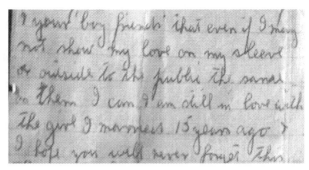

'& your 'boy friends' that even if I may not show my love on my sleeve or outside to the public the same as them I can, I am still in love with the girl I married 15 years ago and I hope you will never forget this'

It appeared his grandfather had also suffered from lack of confidence and shyness, in particular, showing his love and affection for his grandmother in public. Reading these letters for Jerry was somehow like reading about his own life. The feeling low and his life of ground hog days where happiness was all he craved rather than be expected to have a lot of money to provide the best for his family. It appeared he wanted to live life as a Smith, a man for himself, rather than be like other men of the 'Joneses' who were a different class.

Like his grandfather, Jerry wanted to be accepted and loved for who he was, mostly on his own terms, and although he struggled to show appreciation, he knew what it was. Although he struggled to show gratitude, he was grateful beyond words. He knew what it was to be thoughtful and felt Jena had given him a sense of worth and a place in the world that no one had given him before.

As this was new to him, he didn't quite know how to react to her or how to show her his affection, but he certainly knew that Jena had given him the dose of reality he had needed. So Jerry, like his grandfather did almost 80 years ago, decided to put his feelings in writing in his own words.

My sweetest Jena,

Words are hard to describe the feelings I have for you. I admit that I have frustrated you, kept you on a string, at arm's length, pushing and pulling you back and forth, in and out of my life, kept you a secret and invisible in my own reality.

I have been a confused man with not a lot of direction in my life. I have finally looked at that man in the mirror. I sat, and I thought to give up the drink as I wondered what that man in the mirror was thinking of me. I have treated you so poorly, putting others' needs and wants ahead of yours. I have been incredibly selfish with you, and I feel an apology isn't enough.

You have been there for me like no other person in my life, believing in me and helping me realise my worth. You have inspired me, and I have lost sight of what you mean to me. I clearly have disrespected your wants and needs as well as your pure and honest love for me. I have continually put you last as I have been totally engaged with others. I have ignored your needs and felt I have hurt you.

You brought such a bright change to my life, and I have avoided appreciating you and giving you the best, which you deserve. I have been unable to appreciate or be truly grateful towards you as I have been so afraid of my feelings and incredibly fearful of getting close to you, as I find trust a major stumbling block in my life.

I have led you on many times, telling you that you can see something with me in my future, but I have continued to seek out and consider other women. I feel so very ashamed of my behaviour towards you, as it's been all talk and no action on my behalf. I realise keeping you a secret away from my family and friends has been completely disrespectful of me, as you deserve to be acknowledged and not treated as an invisible person.

You have made an amazing impact on my life just by being there for me, and you made me realise that life is not all about work and workmates. There is so much more to life that you have shown me—caring, compassion, dreams, and goals. I have been able to accept your thoughts and ideas of difference and see where I can value myself. I have never felt so appreciated and spoiled in my life since meeting you.

You are a beautiful inspiration in my life, and you gave me the jolt into reality I really needed, which has been missing in my life for so long. I never believed until recently that anyone could help me see that taking baby steps towards change would and could have such an amazing impact. I not only know this I feel it.

You have taught me freedom in our togetherness, and you are my queen of hope and cherub of change. I haven't been able to tell you until now, as I feel I have been foolish and not seen how wonderful you have made my life. I have given my time to the people who are superficial in my life and not you, the purest soul I've met.

I want to shower you with rose petals, soak with you in a bathtub, rub your shoulders and neck, and treat you like you have treated me. If you will have me now after all the waiting you have done and after all the effort you have put in as well as all the unconditional love you have given me, I want to be with you today, tomorrow, and always. If I could choose you to be the one, we would never come undone.

If I could choose . . .

If I could choose to be your light
I would shine on you at night
If I could choose to be your heart
I would beat faster when we're apart
If I could choose to be your pillow
I would snuggle you head to toe.

If I could choose to warm you up
I would overflow your cup
If I could choose to be your pain
You would never hurt again
If I could choose to be your tears
I would conquer all your fears
If I could choose to be your touch
You would feel alive so much
If I could choose you to be the one
We would never come undone.

Hearts and souls like ours belong together.
You are my gold in a coalmine.

All my love, Jerry xxx

Jena knew that Jerry was able to awaken her inner shyness, and she could burst into sharing naughty, nice, and everything in between at any moment with him. She felt he, too, could be just as comfortable releasing his own inhibitions and thoughts with her like no one else had done. She realised he hadn't known affection like she had given him. Therefore, being so new, it was foreign for him to prove anything to anyone. Jena accepted him as he was. He had brought out that brighter sunshine in her smile and that extra spring in her step. They complemented each other with their own personal characters, values, similarities, and differences. Neither of them had ever met someone who they could compare each other to. They could see all sorts of people and no matter who they were, what they said, how much they earned, where

Sensuous Soul

My breath my bond my blossoming beauty
My dream my desire my delightful destiny
My guide my growth my glowing gem
My spirit my style my sensuous soul-mate

My heart my hope my handsome hero
My laugh my lust my love of my life
My nature my nurture my new never-ending
My spirit my style my sensuous soul-mate

My ruby my rock my reverie richness
My taste my touch my true tenderness
My fate my fortune my faith forever
My spirit my style my sensuous soul-mate

they lived, no one had captured their attention quite like they had with each other. No one quite had the charm or magnetism they shared. No one had made them laugh as genuinely or wholeheartedly and no one had brought the intimacy and sensuality to each of them quite like they had with each other. Nothing or no one could compare with their unique closeness with shared dreams and shattered pasts that seemed to link them to each other's souls.

Their sex in the suburbs had become so much more to both of them—a freedom in togetherness. In an instant, they had both turned from nobody to somebody to each other. Whether a moment or a memory, in the end, for Jena, it was about the experience of knowing Jerry in ways that no one else had known. Sex and the suburbs brought two people together for a reason. Sex is the most natural thing in the world to do, and the suburbs is where we all live our lives just like the Smiths and the Joneses—sex and the suburbs, bringing nature and nurture together as one. Never Say Never.

Freedom lies within our heart.
Adjoining souls we'll never part.
Together, we shall bring our love
From inside out and up above.

Freedom rises like the sun
And warms us when we come undone,
Reflects a ray of beaming light,
Rises up, just like a kite.

Freedom brings a calming sense.
With each breath we are not tense.
Courage grows, and wisdom follows,
Uniting strength for all tomorrows.

Freedom's passion delivers wonder
On the inner and deeply under.
Its spirit climbs for us to give
Our love to others, while we live.

The sun for the moon,
The power for the strength,
The armour for the courage,
The kin for the ship.

Freedom sets upon the brave
Eternal existence beyond the grave.
Freedom lies within our heart.
Adjoining souls we'll never part.